SYMPATHETIC PEOPLE

DONNA BAIER STEIN

SYMPATHETIC PEOPLE

DONNA BAIER STEIN

SERVING HOUSE BOOKS

Sympathetic People

ISBN: 978-0-9858495-8-0

Cover art: "An Evening Miracle" by Alexandra Eldridge

Cover design by Allen Mohr

Serving House Books logo by Barry Lereng Wilmont

Published by Serving House Books, LLC
Copenhagen, Denmark and Florham Park, NJ

www.servinghousebooks.com

First Serving House Books Edition 2013

What I've learned about sympathy,
and how much we are all deserving of it,
I've learned from those who have loved me best:
Dorothy, Martin, Jon and Sarah

ACKNOWLEDGEMENTS

"The Great Drawing Board in the Sky," *Prairie Schooner.*

"Coming Clean," *The Literary Review.*

"El Niño," *The Florida Review.*

"Hindsight," *Kansas Quarterly.* First Place Fiction Prize.

"In Heraklion," *G.W. Review.*

"The Jewel Box," *Paterson Literary Review.*

"Lambada," *The South Carolina Review.*

"The Secrets of Snakes," *The Florida Review.* First Place Prize in Fiction Judged by Stephen Dixon.

"Whatever You Want," Published as "Smoke." *Santa Clara Review.*

"The Yogi and the Peacock," *The G. W. Review.*

"Versions," *The G.W. Review.*

"The Second Time the Bird Escaped," *Licking River Review.*

"News Feed," *The Southampton Review.*

"My Lovers #1-5, or Why I Hate Kenny Rogers," *New Ohio Review.*

An earlier version of this collection was a Finalist in the Iowa Fiction Awards.

TABLE OF CONTENTS

VERSIONS

We are all sympathetic people. Individually, or two-by-two. None of us has ever refused a frantic midnight call from a witch-held friend, sat while a pearl-haired senior stood in the aisle of a bus, or shoplifted anything but books, and that was many years ago.

We are rich, at least Harry and I are. Harry (my Hirsute Doll) and I live in a huge (five bedrooms with pool) ranch house in Plano, just outside of Dallas. About twenty minutes from Nieman-Marcus. I may not get elephants in my mailbox, but I do get a plethora of mail-order catalogs. Try as I may, I can't resist going through them as soon as they slide through the slot on the front door.

I was flipping through one's glossy, four-color pages the night Harry called from the clinic to say Nina was coming by to "pick up some of her things."

I was surprised. Other than the massive, silent kiln crowding the washing machine in the basement, I didn't think Nina still had anything in the house. I had cleaned every closet, gone through every room in a fastidious campaign in the eight months Harry and I had been married.

"I better start drinking now," I laughed.

I am thirty-two; every birthday since my eighteenth has surprised me. Harry is thirty-five, for real. Gray is just beginning to fleck his black beard. He has run his own orthopedic practice for five years now—setting fractures, correcting clubfeet and bowlegs, straightening spines in Plaster of Paris jackets.

"I'll come home as soon as I finish up," he promised. He so often came home late.

I hung up the wall phone in the newly redecorated kitchen—we'd put in a Jenn-Air and a pastry island. I poured Scotch, checked my watch, sat down to wait in the living room.

Harry's success and his busy schedule are well deserved after eight long years in medical school, and a residency at the Good Sam Hospital in Phoenix. I didn't know Harry then; Nina shared those lean, Kraft macaroni years. I don't know why Nina left when she did, just when Harry's income started snowballing. But she did leave.

Sometimes—maybe four or six times since we've been married—Harry does something that scares me and I run out of whatever room we are in, grab a phone book and search the Yellow Pages for a nearby motel where I can spend the night. The few friends we have here belong to both of us, and are, in fact, more Harry's friends than mine. Any girlfriends who would understand my coming for just one night live far away. I never end up going to the motel anyway. Those times, usually prompted by one of Harry's loud and frightening rages at how he can't *mold* life the way he molds hips and legs, I can see why Nina ran out on him, but usually I don't understand it.

Nina and I didn't overlap in Harry's life for even a day. A clean break like that meant no catfights, no verbal sniping at *The Other Woman*. In fact, I often liked to think Nina and I might have been friends.

There were no children, although Harry told me they had tried to conceive about a year before Nina left him for her dulcimer-making lover. Instead of remodeling the kitchen, or putting in a pool like most strained couples around here, they hoped their own lucky talisman of renewal might be clutched in a baby's dimpled hand.

Harry and I were still trying to decide whether or not we wanted a family. Harry works hard, for very long hours, and requires constant attention when he's not at the clinic. I imagine, deep down, he worries a child might take me away from him. He's never said that out loud, but I suspect that's one reason he doesn't push me to have one.

I smoked an Ultra-Light, then washed the ashtray and hid the pack of cigarettes. Harry thinks I've quit.

When I heard Harry's BMW pull in the driveway, I met him at the door and after we kissed, we walked upstairs together so Harry could shower.

I stood in the bathroom looking at the fogged-up mirror. I had to shout to be heard above the water; Harry likes the nozzle set on high massage.

"Why didn't you have kids?"

"I've already told you."

"Tell me again. I forgot."

"Because Nina would get one of her sinus headaches every time it came up. Because, by the end, we were making love only after big fights. It was *greedy*, like we were trying to *feel* each other, trying to remember who this person we'd been married to for ten years really was."

"Oh."

"Don't be silly."

Harry stepped out of the shower, dripping water onto the carpet. He kissed the back of my head.

"What about the house?"

"What about it?" Harry put on his big terrycloth robe and wiped the mirror clear with one sleeve.

In the mirror, we were about the same height, but Harry was dark, with a year-round tan, and I was slightly sallow. I had short hair after many years with it down to my waist. I looked unfamiliar; Harry looked protective.

"I don't know. I don't want her to feel bad. Everything's different. The kitchen, the bedroom. The Oriental."

"You worry too much. Don't worry; she'll like you. You'll like each other."

Harry went into the bedroom to dress. I sat down on the sitting room chaise, another new addition, with my elbows on my knees.

"So where's she moving to?"

"Didn't I tell you? San Francisco. She's going to San Francisco to set up some sort of gallery or workshop or something. She leaves next month." Harry pulled on his chinos. "Don't you still know people there?" he asked.

I went to art school in San Francisco. I studied painting there. I met my first boyfriend, David, there.

"What are you smiling about?"

"Just thinking. I know lots of people there. Wonderful people." I sat up. "It'll be perfect. Yes, I can tell Nina about those people; they'll take her in."

I stood up and rifled through a drawer in the desk then pulled out my address book. Almost every name in it was followed by a long list of scratched-out residences.

I did know people in San Francisco, people who'd be happy for a chance to retrieve and wipe clean some dusty vision of themselves from the sixties. People who wouldn't bat an eye at my request that they host and protect my husband's first wife. The people I know in San Francisco are special—artists, photographers, beer drinkers all—and I'd spent many heady hours with them in the kind of conversations nobody seems to find time for anymore.

Six months before David and I broke up, we were drinking beer in a neighborhood bar called the Catfish. We were celebrating the completion of David's dissertation, on Unamuno's "saving incertitude."

"Dad's just offered me a job," David said.

His father marketed a special kind of TV antenna.

"Look, I can't make it as a philosopher. The standards are too high. I'm going to take it."

I lit Kools, one after the other, while David wondered out loud if he might find a happy medium in the family company. He talked about the parallels of transmitting information, the sensitivity to distant messages, the receptivity to truth.

I told him how I thought my art was very different from his philosophy.

"When they come at all," I said, "my paintings stream out of me. You've seen that happen. Maybe," I said, licking foam from my lip, "it's that unselfconscious process that counts."

I tell him that for me, his philosophy and his antennae sound like rugged outcrops of rock, standing far out in one of the polar seas, while my paintings are like the temporary, blazing hibiscus that grow along the roads on the islands.

"You're a child," he said.

Even after we parted, when David would hear from friends about my latest catastrophe—like carrying $600 in cash for a rental deposit, and losing it to a Chinatown pickpocket—he would call to remind me just how naïve I am, how totally unequipped to deal with the real world. Every call confirmed my sense that the break-up had been for the best. I figured I didn't need a scratched and stuck record, like one of my father's old Mills Brothers, telling me what I already knew.

In the sitting room, Scotch at my elbow, I started copying the names and addresses of people I still knew in San Francisco.

"Katy—she'll save wandering cats, hearts, anything. Abby, prowling thrift shops. Chris with his board games, Matt with his basketball..."

I felt overwhelmed. I couldn't write it all down, so I underlined two, three times, and wrote in all capitals.

I listed places where Nina should eat, drink, and look for apartments. I filled both sides of one sheet of paper and at the bottom, printed: *Nina, when you get to S.F., please call these people. They'll help you find an apartment, feed you, keep you happy. They're good people.*

The doorbell rang. I followed Harry's chinos downstairs to the front door.

Nina had a huge frizzy halo of black hair, a corduroy jacket, and, on her feet, striped wool socks in leather sandals. She looked confident.

The three of us stood there smiling and saying too many *hellos* until Harry, always the fixer, said, "Nina, come on in. Let's get out of the hallway. How about a drink? Bloody Mary? Or a vodka tonic?"

"Juice," Nina said, walking into the kitchen. "I haven't touched alcohol since I discovered *shodi*."

"*Shodi*?" I asked, smiling.

"Japanese tea ceremonies. I even make my own pots and cups. Better than yoga."

"That ratty old leotard." Harry laughed, reaching toward the refrigerator.

"Harry, wait." I couldn't remember if Nina had said what she wanted. "We don't have any grapefruit juice because you finished it this morning. Remember?"

"Don't worry," Nina said, smiling at Harry and looking around the room. "You've certainly done a lot in here, haven't you?"

I nodded. "Let's go sit in the living room."

We walked in and positioned ourselves: Harry and me at opposite ends of the couch, Nina in the chair by the fireplace.

"So you make teapots?" I asked.

"Among other things. Lately I've been working with *graffito*."

"What's that?" Harry asked, crossing his legs to take up more space on the couch.

"It's a technique, with a brown glaze. When I scratch a design on the glaze, the natural clay underneath shows through. I've been working a lot lately, using the kiln at school. With the move, I want my own back."

"You've got all those dyes down there, too, you know," Harry said.

"I know. I'll get it all. And that drafting table, the one Pop gave us when you started school. And the propane lamp."

"Sure, sure," Harry said, gulping his Campari. "I forgot that was yours."

"And the gas grill."

"Now wait a sec," Harry said. "That's not yours. I had that before. Didn't I?"

"No. We got it the summer of the Sparlings. It's on the divorce agreement as mine. Take a look."

"Hell, it's fine. I really don't care."

Nina walked over to a small rug I'd moved from the den to put under the piano bench. She started laughing, hands in her front pockets, neck stretched back and loose.

"I thought something looked weird," she said. "You've got the damn thing upside down."

She flipped the rug over.

"It is?" I asked, walking over to her. "Oh lord, you're right. Now it looks like something."

Nina turned to Harry. "What vacation is this from anyway? Is it mine?"

"Oh, no you don't," Harry said. "That I know belongs to me." He stood up. "Anybody else ready for a refill?"

When Harry walked out of the room, Nina picked up a little box she'd been staring at on the bookshelf.

"What's this?" she asked. "*Segillet*? Why do you have this?"

"I was on a dig. Many years ago. In France. Those are little shards of pottery, *segillet*, you're right."

"Ah, digging up the past…" Nina turned away from the bookcase and looked at me.

"Do you still paint?" She sat down. "When Harry first met you, he told me you were pretty good."

"I don't do much these days," I said. "I feel busy with the house. With Harry. I mean to go back to it, but I don't."

She shrugged.

"So, Harry," she said, as he walked back into the room. "What about you? What keeps you busy?"

"Well, actually, I've got a pretty interesting case right now. A bone graft. It's tricky. It's to stabilize a joint in a young woman's leg. The graft has to be accurately fitted. First we'll remove a normal bone, then dovetail it to the defect. It's really a case of the body providing its own best cure, though by fairly violent and dramatic means."

I looked over at Nina to see if she minded hearing the graphic details.

"Listen," I said. "I made you this list." I held out the sheet of paper I'd covered with writing.

Nina raised her eyebrows and took the list from my hand.

"They're old friends of mine. I thought you wouldn't know anyone when you move. I want you to meet them…" I stood waiting.

"Sure, thanks." Nina stuck the list in her pocket. "I'll take it. Doubt I'll have time to call, but I'll take it."

"Nina's pretty good on her own," Harry said. "Remember that time, going to Mendocino? When was it, summer of '65?"

Nina laughed.

"Sure. Driving all the way from Edison, New Jersey, to Mendocino,

California in a Day-Glo van. *A Day-Glo van.*" Nina sat back in her chair. "You were already a budding compulsive at nineteen." She looked over at me. "Harry drove 800 miles our first day out. Then, he fell asleep on a mattress we'd set up in the back."

"When I woke up," Harry interrupted. "Nina was at the wheel. There we were, cruising down the highway at 75 or so!" Harry and Nina laughed.

"That was the first time she'd ever touched a stick shift!" Harry said to me, still laughing.

They talked more about people they both knew. I kept wanting Harry to leave the room again so I could talk to Nina alone. I stared at her while they talked, wanting to hear more about her pottery, her tea ceremonies, wanting to talk about my paintings.

After a while, Nina said, "I'd better be going. I've got to meet someone."

"Let's go get your stuff," Harry said. "Most of it should be together."

We all walked down to the basement. In the laundry room on a bookshelf lining one wall, there were maybe a dozen heavy brown paper bags with mysterious labels: $2PbCO3*Pb3(OH)2$, 25 lbs flint, Copper Carb. On another shelf, there were two dozen large jars, again labeled and filled with colored powders: Cornwall Stone, Ilmenite, Zircopax. Boxes of cones to test the heat in the kiln, and plastic bags filled with dried clay. A thick slab of Plaster of Paris sat on top of a table next to the kiln.

Loading our arms, we each made several trips out to the pick-up Nina had borrowed from a friend. The kiln was lighter than it looked; Harry and Nina together managed to get it up the stairs and into the truck.

We went into the den for the drafting table. Harry wanted to take the whole thing out in one trip. Nina and I both said we thought it wouldn't fit through the door. Harry tried his way, without any luck. Then Nina and I unscrewed the legs and carried the pieces out to the pick-up.

Harry went to wash his hands and Nina and I walked back into the hall.

"There's one other thing," Nina said. "A lace tablecloth my Gramma Rose made."

"I haven't seen anything like that," I said. "I know. I would remember."

Nina looked like she wanted to touch things in the closet, move blankets, picture books, but she closed the door and looked into the living room instead.

"If I see it, I'll mail it," I promised. "It's just that I've gone through everything. I would have seen it."

Harry came in with the lamp and grill, and he and Nina walked outside to put them in the truck. I stayed inside, sitting at the shiny-topped new rosewood dining table, and waited for them to come back.

Then I realized Nina was leaving.

I heard her say goodbye to Harry, then the pick-up door slam, and the tires crunch over the gravel in the driveway.

There's a yellow light a few yards down the street from our house. A traffic warning that flashes all night. First the top bulb flashes, then the bottom, casting alternating circles of a golden glow on the sidewalk and the grass. I stared at the light and wished I could levitate the list I'd written so carefully out of Nina's pocket and back into my own hands.

There's a version of me that David knows: surrounded by untaped but still packed cartons of brushes, jars and books. I stand in paint-smeared jeans and a dirty smock, twisting and sucking on a strand of hair, staring at a blank canvas.

There is a version of me that Harry knows: sitting on our Chinese rug in front of our fireplace, flipping through catalogs, filling out order forms for crystal door knobs and brass letter holders, waiting for replies.

There is Harry's vision of Nina driving down the highway, a phosphorescent cannon forever heading west. There is my vision of Nina pulling out of the driveway, her hands on the wheel bathed in on-again, off-again gold.

There are visions and versions of people all over the place.

Whatever the reason, sitting there at that table, hearing the truck door slam, watching the yellow lights in eternal indecision, I knew that I'd lost something.

THE SECRETS OF SNAKES

The night before her son left for spring-break camp, he warned Arlene that his pet snake, a Northern black racer, would soon begin molting. The skin had become dull and milky, and even the scale on the eye, which was round and usually clear like a built-in contact lens, had clouded. Mark told her the snake would be partly blind the first few days she'd be taking care of it. Then, three or four days after its eyes cleared, it would shed its skin.

Next morning she drove Mark to the camp bus, piling his duffel bag and acoustic guitar in the trunk of the Explorer. As soon as she returned home, she went right to his room—a lively, sometimes puzzling mix of Larry Bird and Red Hot Chili Peppers posters; Ninja Turtle action figures and model airplanes; shoe boxes filled with baseball cards, key chains, seashells. A Red Ryder toy rifle that had belonged to Arlene's father leaned against one corner next to two golf clubs that needed re-gripping. An X-Men comic book lay open on Mark's desk.

A female character stood in the first oversize panel, arms akimbo and legs spread. Raven-haired. Impossible breasts. Thigh-high boots. And what Arlene's mother used to call a wasp waist, cinched in a bright red belt.

Tomorrow, Arlene would have the opportunity--if that's really what one wanted to call it--to make love with someone other than her husband. She hadn't decided what she would do, but she found she liked the sharp-edged ambivalence.

Imagining this man touching her enlivened her. At work, the air between them was so charged she felt certain their colleagues at the hospital could see it pulse. Thinking about his invitation to lunch, and what it might lead to, Arlene ran her tongue over her lip, then turned to the cage and bent to look at Mark's snake.

The scales on its back, overlapped like shingles on a roof, were dry and silky as patent leather. There were small tears in the skin around its lips.

With his father's help, Mark had converted an aquarium into a cage, using tight-fitting plywood to replace one broken side and framing the top with wood. This top was secured with angled hinges and covered with quarter-inch wire net and fiberglass screen. Right before boarding the bus that morning, Mark reminded Arlene, with the condescension of a smart nine-year-old, first that it was her idea that he go to camp, and second that she must always replace the fiberglass screen, or his snake could get out.

At first, Arlene had been repulsed by the snake. Mark had to lobby hard. But after it had lived with them a month, she realized it was clean and really quite beautiful. And all she had to do while Mark was away was keep the cage clean and dry and fill the water dish, a large tip-proof plastic bowl. She was to feed the snake regularly—raw chicken, the bony tips of chicken wings, thin strips of beef heart dropped through the wire net. Mark had shown her how to approach the snake. Slowly, so as not to startle it. Otherwise, he said, even though the snake's vision was bad, it would sense movement, hiss, vibrate its tail and strike. But he reassured her it was not venomous.

She fed it raw chicken then ran herself a bath, pouring in mineral salt from the Dead Sea. She lay in the tub for half an hour. Her younger daughter Ellie had spent the night at a friend's across town, so the house was empty and blessedly quiet. Slipping down into the water so her ears were submerged, Arlene felt the pulsing current beneath everything. The dark berries of her nipples poked above the water; below its surface, the bikini scar from her c-section rippled. She opened her legs, started to imagine this new man sliding into her.

She startled when the phone rang, splashing water all over the floor.

"Arlene?"

She stood in the hall, wrapped in a towel.

"Hi." The smile rose from deep inside her.

"I told you I'd call," he said.

"I'm glad you did."

She could hear someone talking behind him, probably a nurse. She wondered if it was someone from her rotation and felt flooded with guilt.

Still, nothing at all had happened between them. Not really.

"Would you have lunch with me?" he asked.

"I can't," she said, sounding firmer than she felt. "I've got to pick up Ellie at noon."

The silence on the other end of the phone made Arlene worry she'd made a mistake. She'd already, in her mind, picked out a dress to wear and knew that, if she accepted his invitation, she would wear her best underwear.

And anyway, what was wrong with having lunch? She could stop things at any time, not let them get out of hand.

"Would tomorrow work instead?" she asked.

"That'd be great."

Then, stupidly, she said, "I'll meet you at the Landfall at noon." Why on earth had she chosen a restaurant she'd often gone to with her husband Daniel?

She knew how much strength her family gave her. It wasn't that Arlene had never thought about getting divorced. But she couldn't imagine it, not really. Both her marriage and her children were hard-won prizes, prayers that had been answered.

And Daniel was her most intimate and intelligent friend. He mostly seemed to adore her, except for the times he screamed obscenities at her or the children, frightening them all. Or when he immersed himself in work so much so she felt invisible. These were times she didn't love him. But she always thought the most recent bout of rage would be the last one and that one day, the stress of his demanding job would be behind them.

On the second morning of her snake care duties, Arlene was supposed to change the newspapers lining the bottom of the cage. This was the task that most frightened her. She decided to do it early, after Daniel left for work but while Ellie still slept.

She walked into Mark's room in her nightgown. It had red hearts and red birds between blue stripes, and it covered her from neck to ankles. This irritated Daniel.

Mark and Daniel had caulked the edges of the aquarium with silicone seal and installed a shoebox where the snake could curl and hide. The snake was in there now.

The door at the top of the cage had a hinge and latch; Arlene had to yank to pull it open. Then she picked up a forked finger-thick sapling Mark had left beside the cage. Pushing up the sleeves of her gown, she reached inside and pinned the snake behind its head. She held her breath, reached in, and grabbed its neck. The animal remained surprisingly still. She dropped the stick, took hold of the snake further down its body, then picked it up and dropped it into the opened burlap collecting bag on the floor. Without looking inside, she tied a firm knot at the top of the bag. She changed the newspapers, untied the knot and, holding the bag upside down, let the snake slide gently back into its home.

The restaurant was five miles from the hospital where they both worked in Falmouth. When Arlene entered and saw him at the table, she felt a rush of desire that was very different from the sometimes unthinking attachment she had to Daniel.

She left most of her lunch uneaten on her plate. When he said, "I know I shouldn't do this, but do you think we could go somewhere we could be alone?" she nodded. If she didn't speak, it might lessen her complicity.

They stood behind his car in the parking lot. He pulled her so close to him she could feel the bulge in his pants and smell the mix of cedar and lemon in his after shave.

After a deep kiss interrupted by the sound of someone's car alarm going off—and a promise they would meet again, soon, they parted ways.

Arlene drove home feeling transcendent, almost physically pierced by the beauty of the world. A minnow of guilt swam in her brain, but she ignored it.

But as soon as she walked up the stairs in her house, she felt a sudden panic that something might have happened to Mark's pet while she'd been gone. She paid the babysitter quickly, sat Ellie down in front of the television in the master bedroom, and ran into Mark's room to make sure everything was all right.

The snake lay coiled just outside the shoe box. When she saw that things looked normal, she put her hands on her hips and let herself enjoy the memory of what had just happened and the anticipation of what might be yet to come.

She was proud of the way she had handled lunch. Yes, they had kissed. Yes, she had felt a wonderful new charge of wanting. But nothing more had happened. She could hold her head high.

In addition, she was proud of the way she had conquered her fear of Mark's snake! The racer had obviously learned that Arlene was its new food source, and when Arlene tapped the cage, it came forward and waited for her offering. It raised itself up and, through the wire cover, took a strip of beef heart directly from Arlene's fingers.

Arlene had seen Mark offer the snake his outstretched palm while he was training it, so it could test with its tongue where the skin was too tight to bite. She had watched Mark handle the snake, holding it firmly but not so hard that the animal was injured.

That night, after Arlene and Ellie had eaten dinner alone—Daniel once again held up late at the office—Arlene tucked her daughter into bed then walked into Mark's room. With a new certainty, she lifted and held the snake herself. Even though its head twisted and thrashed at first, the animal finally calmed down. This new and unexpected skill brought her a rush of confidence.

Saturday morning, five days after Mark had gone to camp, Daniel announced that Marie, a young woman he'd once worked with at the

Oceanographic Institute, was back in Woods Hole for a brief visit. He'd suggested she stop by for lunch the next day. Arlene was not to worry; he would handle all the preparations himself.

On Sunday, Arlene almost missed church. She lay in bed late, trying to figure out whether or not she should free up time during the coming week to go for another lunch, realizing that repeating the illicit meeting was probably asking for trouble. When she saw that it was almost eight, she poked Daniel.

"I'm late." She jumped out of bed, avoiding his face for fear he would see what she'd been thinking.

But Daniel only rolled over, annoyed at having his sleep disturbed.

"Ellie's still in bed," she said. "Feed her breakfast, but don't let her watch TV all morning, will you?"

Daniel groaned, and Arlene took this for a yes.

The sermon that morning was about sacrifice and how God sometimes asks us to do something that doesn't make sense. The sermon comforted her, and she sat in the wooden pew feeling both blessed by the love of God and unusually seductive. This feeling stayed with her the entire drive home.

At home, Daniel had set four place settings on the butcher block table in the kitchen. He'd brought curried chicken and palak paneer from a nearby restaurant and moved these from their plastic containers into white earthenware bowls. A bottle of wine stood in a double-walled cylindrical cooler.

Arlene, not wanting to lose the pleasant feeling she'd brought home from church, decided she'd forego wine and made a show of bringing a carton of juice to set on the table.

Daniel said, "Marie'll be here soon."

He didn't look at her when he spoke, but then he hadn't looked at her much that week at all. He'd been busy at work, staying late every night and Arlene knew that *he* knew she was annoyed by this.

Arlene put her hands around his waist and turned him away from the counter to face her. She hugged him, grateful for his strong shoulders and familiar Givenchy aftershave. She initiated a kiss, something she knew she did too rarely. This time, it was Daniel who was preoccupied.

"Thanks." He pecked at her lips, smiled briefly, and turned back to preparing the rice. "I don't want this to overcook," he said. "We need a real rice cooker."

Just then the doorbell rang.

Arlene hadn't really remembered which of Daniel's colleagues Marie was, but when she opened the door, she recognized the young woman's curly blond hair and slim figure right away. There were re-introductions, a handing-over of Marie's suede jacket, then, after a quick tour of the house, Arlene called Ellie to join them, and the four sat down to lunch.

Arlene stuck to her resolution to drink juice, but Daniel and Marie emptied the bottle of wine quickly. She was relieved to see Ellie behave beautifully at the table and when her daughter asked to leave, she said, "Of course. Run upstairs and watch TV in Mommy and Daddy's bedroom."

Arlene remembered that at last year's Christmas party, Marie had come with a white-shirted scientist with rimless glasses and a ponytail. She'd danced provocatively whenever she and her partner neared Arlene and Daniel. At the time, Arlene wondered if her husband could be having an affair. He flirted with other women outrageously, right in front of her.

As usual, Daniel dominated the conversation—talking about the projects he was working on, about people he and Marie both knew. Neither made much of an effort to include Arlene in the conversation. Still, Arlene was happy to have her as a visitor on what would otherwise have been a boring Sunday afternoon. She liked Marie—her earnestness, the envious way she looked at the photos of Mark and Ellie on the refrigerator, the way she let Arlene know without even speaking of it, that she didn't want to live alone much longer.

After they ate, Arlene suggested that Daniel and Marie go sit in the living room, and she would bring in tea. Waiting for the kettle, Arlene listened for Marie's spirited but also ingratiating laugh.

When the tea had steeped, Arlene took a tray with cups into the living room.

"So," Daniel was saying, "the sea slug bites the poisonous tentacles off the anemone and coats them with mucus so he can swallow them without danger. Later, he may even put some of the newly-acquired poison on his own back to protect himself."

Arlene watched the intent way Marie listened to him, unblinking and encouraging even in her silence. It was a habit Arlene had lost during the years she'd spent with Daniel.

"Bruce and Jelle finished their research on the catfish." Marie now worked for the National Marine Fisheries Service and had just returned from a research voyage. "Finding out why it needs so many sense organs."

Daniel shook his head, impatient. He'd heard this bit of news.

Marie looked disappointed.

"What will you do now, Marie?" Arlene asked quickly. She tried to make other people, strangers, comfortable, even when she was not.

"I don't know yet." Marie seemed grateful. "I'm bored and want something different. Isabelle's organizing an expedition to the Galapagos Rift Vents. Maybe I'll go."

"Do you want to go?"

"No, not really. Isabelle's a pain, an egomaniac. And I'm tired of traveling."

"Maybe Daniel could find you something again at the Institute." For a moment Arlene pictured the four of them in ten years, Marie and Daniel married, Arlene with her potential lover, and all of them, even the children, happy. Momentarily buoyed, she pictured them all journeying toward some greater good, guided by unseen hands.

Daniel sank further into his chair, comfortable at last with the mix of wine and tea. Marie mirrored his shift in position.

"Oh!" Arlene cried. "I've completely forgotten it!"

Daniel squinted at her.

"Mark's snake," she said. "I forgot to feed it this morning."

"Oh," Daniel and Marie said in unison.

Arlene stood, heading toward the stairs, talking over her shoulder as she went, "I'll be right back."

When Arlene entered Mark's room Ellie joined her. "I'm bored!" she whined.

Arlene looked at the snake, which had curled up in the water bowl, soaking its skin.

"Look, Ellie," she said, trying to remove her daughter's hand from her skirt. "The eye—it's starting to clear."

She walked over to check the temperature on the thermometer hanging at the side of the cage–76 degrees. Just right. She wanted to show Ellie how easily she could hold the snake. But when she moved to undo the latch, Ellie hid behind her, squealing. "Mommy, don't! It's dangerous!"

"It's okay, Ellie. I know how to do it," Arlene reassured her. "Mark showed me. Look."

And she used the sapling again to pin the snake's head to the floor of the cage. This time, the snake moved, but Arlene went ahead and took hold of it but too far down. When she lifted it, it turned its head and bit the fleshy side of her hand.

Ellie's mouth dropped open.

Arlene tried to shake the snake loose, even tried to smile at her daughter, but the thing wouldn't let go.

"Mommy!" Tears filled Ellie's eyes.

"It's okay, Ellie. Mommy's going to be okay." Arlene looked around the room. Her own eyes began to water. Then she started toward the door, snake still dangling from her left hand, its fangs still in place while she held its curled body in her right. She took one step at a time as though she were walking through deep water. Her hand ached where the snake's fangs had punctured her skin. "We need Daddy," she said.

Still holding the snake and with a soft moan of horror at how heavy and limp it felt, she ran to the top of the stairs.

"Daniel!"

He came from the living room and stood gaping up at her. The snake's jaws were still clamped around her flesh, and its thin body writhed in the air beneath her arm.

Marie had followed right behind him. "Oh my God," she said.

"It's okay," Daniel said, but he didn't start to climb up to her. "Arlene, you're going to be all right." He glanced at Marie as though she could handle this then turned back to look up at Arlene. "You've got to let go of it," he said softly. "Its teeth are curved backwards. If you don't ease the jaws off carefully, the teeth will be torn out. And your wound will be deeper."

Arlene had really started to cry now, but just as suddenly as the snake had bit her, it let go and fell to the floor. It seemed to take forever, but Daniel finally climbed the stairs and reached them. Daniel scooped the snake up off the floor and disappeared into Mark's room. He came back empty-handed.

"We've got to get you to a doctor," he said. "I'll take you."

"No." Arlene looked at her hand. "I'm okay. It's not venomous. Mark told me. You told me. It's just a silly little snake."

"But you should have somebody look at it," Marie said.

"No. I mean yes, I will. I'll go. But you stay here with Ellie. I'll just drive down to the clinic. It's not far. I'll be back, and then we can finish our tea." Arlene was trying to stop crying. By now, her hand didn't even hurt. A scratch from a cat she'd owned once had been far more painful. "I don't want you to come with me," she said.

But Daniel pushed her into the bathroom and washed her hand with soap. He wiped it with antiseptic. The teeth marks made a U-shaped pattern.

"In a few hours," Daniel said, "you'll hardly see the marks."

Arlene just sniffled.

He insisted on driving, and when she climbed into the seat beside him she stared out the window, refusing to look at him.

"Maybe I shouldn't even go," she muttered. "You shouldn't leave your guest."

"Marie'll be fine," Daniel said, steering the car down the driveway. She could see Marie and Ellie standing at the dining room windows, watching them go. Marie had her hand on Ellie's shoulder.

Daniel pushed her ahead of him through the rotating door into the clinic.

One of the doctors she knew happened to be on call. He'd treated Mark for a dislocated shoulder once. He was probably ten years younger than she was, with red hair that brushed the collar of his white coat.

He wanted her up on the examining table. At first, Arlene said no, that wasn't necessary. But Daniel frowned at her. So she climbed up and sat there feeling like a little girl as the doctor rested his hand on her shoulder.

"It's Mrs. Kelly, isn't it? How's your boy? And the hospital, too—I haven't seen you there much lately."

"Uh, yes, Mrs. Kelly," she stuttered. "I mean, Arlene. Mark's fine. This is his father." She pointed vaguely toward Daniel, who was leaning on his elbows next to a jar of tongue depressors. "I'm afraid that I've been bitten by a snake." She clasped her hands together to keep them from shaking then added, "I don't come into the hospital during your shift anymore. Only Mondays and Wednesdays. In the morning."

"Snake, huh?"

"It's a pet," she said. "My son's. It's a racer. I know it's not venomous; we got it from a store, and we looked at the markings in the books. It's a racer."

The young doctor examined her hand while Arlene studied the pale freckled skin on his forehead.

"No fang marks," he said cheerfully, looking up at her with his clear blue eyes. "No swelling. How long ago were you bitten?"

"Maybe half an hour."

"A venomous bite would leave fang marks. Two distinct puncture wounds. Those aren't here."

"Told you," Daniel said.

The doctor ignored him. He was so handsome, Arlene thought. "Did you feel any burning?" he asked.

"No."

"Any dizziness, nausea, shortness of breath?"

Probably loyal and quiet, too.

"No. I mean, I was just sick at the thought of it." Arlene shifted slightly on the table, crossing her legs. Daniel jangled the keys in his pocket impatiently.

"I think you're fine," the doctor said. He patted her hand and Arlene knew she'd been dismissed. "I'll have one of the other nurses clean the wound for you and give you a tetanus shot just for good measure. Then you can go home."

After he left the room, Arlene looked in the silver paper towel dispenser and noticed she needed lipstick.

When they got home, the dishes were cleared from the table and left in neat stacks on the kitchen counter. The leftover Indian food had been covered with saran wrap and put in the refrigerator. Even the wine bottle had been carefully deposited in the recycling basket under the sink.

A note from Marie on the counter explained that Ellie was playing next door with the neighbor children, and Marie herself had gone home. She thanked both Arlene and Daniel for lunch.

"You okay?" Daniel asked.

She hadn't spoken to him during the entire car ride home.

"Yes." She studied his face to see if he'd ask anything else. Her neck and shoulders hurt.

"You sure?" Daniel said.

"Did you ever kiss her?" she asked.

"No." Daniel stuck his hands in his jeans pockets then took them out again. "Did you want me to?"

Arlene didn't know how to answer.

Daniel took her bandaged hand into his own and planted a kiss on it.

That night in bed, Arlene and Daniel made love. Daniel wanted to go a second time, but Arlene said no and turned to lie on her side, looking away from him.

She thought about the impatience of the flesh and the strong lure of the things of this world. When she felt Daniel fall asleep, she turned over to look at his face for a long time. And then she climbed out of their bed.

She turned the light on in Mark's room then walked to the corner where she grabbed one of the golf clubs that leaned there. She took it with her to the cage, opened the hinged door, and scooped up the snake. Mark could have another pet, anything he wanted; she knew how much this one had hurt her. She saw that the skin had already started to peel back off the snake's nose and head.

She dropped it into the burlap bag and silently carried it downstairs and outside.

For a few minutes she stood in her driveway, looking up at the side of her lovely house, at the dark rooms where Ellie and Daniel now slept and at the single bulb that illuminated Mark's posters and, for once, neatly made bed. Even with her flannel nightgown on, she started shaking.

She opened the bag and turned it upside down. The snake dropped down on the asphalt and slithered forward in wavy motions, every part of its body following the same path as its head. Its tongue darted in and out of its mouth, testing the air for smells.

She climbed in the Explorer. She turned on the ignition and headlights, then inched the car forward until she found the snake right in her path. She drove over it once and stopped, mortified at what she had done. Then she put the car in reverse and drove over the snake again and again, until she could finally imagine they were all safe.

COMING CLEAN

What I could do is push through the revolving glass door of his smoky glass building on DuPont Circle. I could walk past the card shop in the lobby where he bought me that pink plastic wind-up birthday cake ten months ago, the day he licked me down there even though I was having my period, and no one had ever done that to me before. It's the same shop where, eight months ago, he bought me a Victorian heart and rose Valentine's Day card that I locked inside the pages of my Bible until August when he performed one of his many disappearing acts and dumped me. In September, another card, in honor of Honey Month—this one with a picture of a trench-coated man standing under a cloud, rain falling on his head, and these words inside, "My therapist says it only seems like the sun's always shining where I'm not standing. But this time I know it's true." Below that, his name in the sharply tilted handwriting I sometimes stare at to see if it holds some key.

Forget your opinions about whether or not I should give this man the time of day. For now, just know that he likes cards. And that this time, I'm not aiming for any Hallmark kind of greeting.

I walk through the lobby, my stacked-heel mules slapping on green marble.

Brass elevator doors slide open; I step inside. My right heel taps nervously on carpet so thick there's no sound. I study my reflection in the mirrored walls. I've worn a dress that shows off my waist. I have a good hair cut from a guy in New York who used to cut Mia Farrow's hair. He's Greek and writes poetry. He layers my hair, makes fancy moves with his scissors so it has body. I can tell that the man who stepped into the elevator behind me thinks I look good. But he's gone by the time we reach the 14th floor.

As soon as the door opens, I've entered a scene I've imagined dozens of times. The carpeted reception area, the crescent-shaped desk with the pretty headphoned receptionist behind it. I've even imagined the crystal vase of flowers and silver bowl of wrapped candies.

The scene's a little different than I expected though. How could it not be? The lighting is brighter, and there are windows that look out on a low-slung drugstore across the street. There's a brown leather couch and four chairs in a seating area off to the right.

I stop for a minute, breathing it all in.

The pretty receptionist lifts her face and repositions the mouthpiece. "Can I help you?" Her smile is framed in dark red.

"Yes." I try to match her wary warmth. "Thank you."

She waits as I step forward. Before that smile can fade, I say quickly, "I'm here to see Todd Siebert."

All wariness disappears. I'm not lost, I'm not selling anything. I'm here to see one of the upstanding lawyers in this upstanding firm.

She fingers one earring. Her nails match the red on her lips. "Is he expecting you?" she asks.

On some level, surely, I think to myself. "Yes."

"Then let me ring his secretary for you, Ms. - ?"

I've spoken to Todd's secretary on the phone maybe a half dozen times. I know her voice well, and she must know mine. At first, I never left my name. By summertime, I started saying it. I know when she went into labor because Todd cancelled one of our infrequent rendezvous. I've wondered if she is partly in love with him because I was Todd's secretary once and know how that felt.

She's never asked what I'm calling about. She simply says, "Can I give you his voice mail?"

Sometimes, worried about the aftermath of an argument, I'd want to ask, "Is he okay? Is he coming into the office?" Once he spent two weeks in bed with depression. It happened after I went to Europe, after one of the many times we broke up. I went without telling him but don't know how much, if anything, that had to do with him falling blue.

When I'd reach Todd's voice mail instead of his secretary, I wouldn't always leave a message. Sometimes, I'd just listen, phone pressed hard against my ear.

"Who can I say is here to see him?" The receptionist's fingers tap her headset. A pearl ring decorates her right hand.

While she speaks my name into the mouthpiece, her eyes are on a *People* magazine. I take the chance to look around. There are no footprints on the carpet, no trace of my path from the elevator. Other magazines fan out on a small table between the chairs, *The Washingtonian*, *Forbes*, *Lawyers Weekly*. The name of the law firm—Redatch, Mull, and Keaveney—appears on the wall in sans serif gold letters.

I don't want to think about how Todd will feel when he learns that I'm here, in the lobby of his office. I would want so much for him to be glad, and maybe a part of him will be. But it will not be a big enough part, and I know that mostly he will be afraid and embarrassed. I can already hear the strained way his voice will come out from the top of his throat when he greets me.

When he steps through an opening in a curved wooden wall, I swallow. My eyes drink him in. The crisp smoothness of his white button-down shirt. The slight sheen of his windowpane tie.

"Hi," he says. Breathless.

I can feel fear coming off him in waves, and it's that fear that I hate, that makes me know he isn't the man I want him to be, and how much I am going to be hurt.

"Hi," I say back.

He has almost reached me now, and his beautiful long fingers fumble in front of him. I can guess what he's thinking: *Do I shake her hand, kiss her cheek, run?*

I decide to make it easy on him and stick my hand out.

"I was in DC for work," I say, "and thought I'd stop by."

"Gee. I."

"I had to be in town, for work, and thought I'd stop by," I stupidly repeat though it's a lie.

"That's great," he says but it doesn't sound like he means it. "I, uh, I've got to go. But. That's great."

This time, I don't give him any relief.

The taupe ground of his tie is flecked with beige and brown. During our infrequent rendezvous, I have untied his ties, unbuckled his belts, lifted his dry-cleaned shirts out of his pants. I have unbuttoned his buttons slowly, relishing each sight of new skin. I have laid my palm on the wonderful bulge in his pants, unzipped him and released him into air.

Now he looks at me helplessly.

What is it I want him to do?

Grab me, kiss me, receptionist be damned? Sit me down on the brown couch and tell me all the failures of connection he's ever made then promise never to make them again?

The silence between us is huge.

These are my choices:

1. I could shout out loud, right here in the lobby of Redatch, Mull, and Keaveney, "I've been having an on-again-off-again affair with you for a year now. What are you going to do about it?" But this doesn't seem a great plan. Partly because the receptionist, who has begun filing her nails with an emery board, isn't a big enough audience.

2. I could take another step closer, hoping Todd will respond to the pheromones that spark such chemistry between us. He's made me come while I lay on a bed, and he sat on a chair fifteen feet away. He's grown hard during phone conversations from opposite coasts.

My eyes are stuck on his. I can't even look at the rest of his body. He clears his throat. "You look great."

3. I could, of course, play it cool a little longer, like I've been doing all these months. I can pretend we're really just friends, because sometimes I think we are that, too.

"There's no problem if you can't join me for lunch," I say.

"What? Wait a minute," Todd says.

The receptionist has given up all pretence of emery-boarding. She knows this is no ordinary law firm lobby encounter. But when I glare at her, her eyes drop back down to the magazine.

I know that after I leave, if I can figure out how to walk out with my dignity, Todd will scurry back to his office, where I imagine he keeps a photograph of his wife, and spend the afternoon in a mild sweat. He will stay torn between wanting to see me and not. Between thinking himself a coward, and grateful he hasn't been caught.

He puts his hands in the air between us, as though they'll be part of our dialogue. I look through the spaces between his fingers.

4. I could, though this isn't like me at all, brush past those hands through the opening in the wall behind him. If my brain were to change its patterns, I might just walk through the opening in that nut-colored wall. I would feel Todd, hear him follow me nervously down the carpeted hall. I would somehow know where his office is. Inside, I would ignore the shelves of leather law books, and make a beeline for the photograph on his desk.

But my brain doesn't change. I don't move.

Todd's hands plunge to his sides.

"I'm not sure about lunch," he says. I know every nuance of his voice, when it wills me closer, or pushes me away.

But I'm only half-listening. In my imagination I'm still back in his office, lifting the framed photograph from the desk, dropping it to the floor, placing my heel on it. The crunch of glass turns my stomach.

Here in the lobby, there's a different sound. The receptionist answers the phone. "Redatch, Mull, and Keaveney," she says, breathless with efficiency. "May I help you?" She puts the call through quickly, as if the receiver burns. It might be someone's wife.

"I just don't think lunch is going to work today." The phone, and the receptionist's competence, have given Todd firm footing now.

My stomach twists seeing all that cracked glass.

I imagine rescuing the photo from the shards. Turning to see the astonished face of the secretary I've talked to, known yet not known, all this time. The young associates who've temporarily stopped lawyering to watch along with the senior partners who mentor Todd. Some will have already feared this scene unfolding in their own offices.

I would hold up the picture to all of them and say, "This is a lie. This picture of family happiness is a lie."

"I've got someone waiting for me," Todd says, his hands deep in his pockets.

The man I've broken a commandment for has become a lawyer again. His shoulders are back, his head high. "Circuit Court papers to file. By five."

To my mind, at least part of the truth lies in what Todd has written to me:

"Making love to you was the best I ever had or dreamt of."
"No one in my life has ever gotten to me the way you do."
"I communicate with you more often, and more deeply, than I do with anyone else."
And more rarely, *"I love you."*

I want to ask the receptionist what she knows about love. Can she separate it from longing? Does she think it's selective, that the light that falls from the sun is discriminatory, or that one human being can be more special than any other?

Take a look at any card store, I want to tell her, you'll see how many different kinds of love have been identified. Perhaps there are even more.

The telephone rings again; both Todd and I jump. The receptionist fumbles as she reaches to answer, but she is a pro. Her voice is friendly, smooth, professional. Even the stranger on the other end of the line seems more a part of Redatch, Mull, and Keaveney than I do.

Todd's hands come out of his pockets and rub down his pant legs. He does nothing to rescue me from the receptionist's stare.

"Lunch is hard right now," he says.

We've joked about the connotations of "hard" before, but not now.

Though I can feel that thread rattling around as another possibility. Reality can change in a heartbeat.

When I don't answer, he repeats himself, "I said going out for lunch is going to be hard right now."

The receptionist, giving up on us, goes back to reading about more moving love affairs.

I look at my watch. 12:15.

He's got a watch on, too. He knows what time it is.

"Lunch would have been nice," I say, clearing my throat and turning away toward the elevator. "But really..." Another page of *People* turns behind me. "What would life be without hunger?"

EL NIÑO

Albert's the boy next door. He likes his stunt bike with its gyro and pegs, has read through Volume 19 of *Goosebumps*, and knows how to do a Cruyff turn in soccer. He can write his name in Egyptian hieroglyphs. And Mrs. Grise knows that his parents are getting divorced.

Yesterday after school, Albert told Mrs. Grise that he had heard a man on TV say El Niño is coming to upset the world. Albert said he'd been eating Cocoa Puffs with milk and a sliced banana for breakfast when the man explained how temperatures in the Pacific Ocean had warmed along the equator.

"That's the red line around the fat part of the globe," Albert had explained.

Mrs. Grise thought of her son, born ten years before Albert, who once asked for a globe for his birthday. She didn't think he'd ever looked at it much, and now, of course, it was too late. Today, she decides, she will throw the globe away along with everything else behind that terrible closed door.

By 3:30 she has accomplished nothing and sits drinking wine in a coffee cup at her kitchen table. She has a fine view of the rectangle of yard that separates her house from her neighbors'. She has not crossed it since her son's death a year ago.

Through her kitchen window she sees Albert suddenly burst through the screen door of his house and run outside toward his new trampoline. His hair sticks out like wayward straw.

Albert climbs the steel two-step ladder and, once aloft, looks down at the round blue ocean of mesh beneath him, bending his knees the way he has learned to in gym. Soon, his bounce is deep and lively. At school, they have warned him that somersaults should never be done without a harness and that spotters should always be present. But his mother is busy putting together a new grill in the driveway. Caesar, the cat, glides through the grass. Beyond them both, through a big window, he watches the neighbor lift her coffee cup to salute him.

El Niño is coming.

Albert's father is coming, too. He is due to pick up Albert and his younger brother and sister, Perry and Angela, in half an hour. They spend every other weekend, every Tuesday from 4:00-7:00, and every other Thursday (when school is half-day) from 12-7:00 with their father, who lives two miles across town in a house smaller than this one.

Albert's mother put together the trampoline all by herself. It's from the Boing, Boing Company in Australia. It's called their Super Bouncer and has eight legs that bend like upside-down croquet hoops and rest on the grass at the side of their house. There's a sandbox there as well, and a three-story fort complete with a "telephone" constructed by Albert's mom of white tubing she found at the lumber store.

"Your mother doesn't own this house, I do," Albert's father has told him more than once.

Albert stops jumping, climbs down the short ladder, and walks over to see the red and black pieces of metal strewn over the driveway. The big box they bought yesterday at Costco (where Perry got lost in the frozen food section and Angela opened a pack of colored pencils that spilled onto the floor) is torn open now, the lowercase letters W-E-B on one piece, and E-R on the other.

Albert knows from the man on TV that El Niño means "the boy." He knows that Peruvian fishermen named it, many years ago, after the Christ child. He knows that now it will bring mudslides and crashing waves in California, dry spells and drought in Australia and Africa.

"What you doing, hon?" Albert's mother asks without looking at him.

"Nothing."

Angela comes through the screen door dragging her *101 Dalmatians* overnight bag behind her, the hem of her nightgown stuck in the zipper.

Two Beanie Babies peek over the edge of the outside pocket.

Angela jerks her head toward Albert and runs to get the plastic golf club propped against the side of the house.

"I don't want to play golf with you now," Albert says. His mother is busy pushing a large bolt into a silver circle and pays no attention.

"Freakazoid," Angela counters, and swings the club inches above Albert's head.

In her kitchen, behind the open window, Mrs. Grise gasps and covers her mouth with her hand. She is seeing her son's head, the blond hair matted with blood.

Albert laughs and grabs the golf club from his sister's hands. Daniel waddles out the screen door, plastic pants low on one hip. Their father's green car pulls into the driveway.

"Freakazoid. Freakazoid. Freakazoid," Angela yells, tugging on the golf club Albert won't release.

Behind him, Albert's mother curses quietly, but Albert pretends not to hear.

"Stop it, Angela," he says, still unsure if he's going to have to give up the club.

Albert's father climbs out of the car, his polio-shrunken arm appearing first. His father was nine, just the age Albert is now, when he woke one morning on his family's Texas farm with a fever and a headache.

Caesar runs over to rub against Albert's father's legs.

"Hi, Kate," Albert's father says to Albert's mother in a tone Albert doesn't want to understand.

"Ron," his mother answers.

"Caesar caught a mouse, Daddy!" Angela shouts, forgetting the golf club. "Its stomach was falling out and Daniel ate it. He said, 'Yum, chocolate.'"

"Angela!"

Albert watches his mother swivel on her heels to frown at Angela. Dropping the golf club, he walks over and abruptly pulls his mother to a standing position. Then he tells Angela to put her bag in the car and goes inside to get his and Daniel's stuff.

Mrs. Grise continues to watch her neighbors standing in the driveway just a few yards from her window. The two grown-ups appear to be arguing, though she cannot hear their voices as well as she had heard the children's. She admires both of Albert's parents. Despite his polio, Ron built up an extremely successful software company. He is kind and gentle with his children. And Kate is smart and strong-willed, and does many of the things, like building that grill, that Mrs. Grise has always depended on her husband to do.

Now, Mr. Grise is hardly ever home. Since the accident, he works long hours and travels a great deal on company business. When she sees him, they rarely speak; both are so afraid whatever words they choose to say might push the other to a final break.

Suddenly, Mrs. Grise sees Albert's mother push Albert's father, and he falls to the ground. When he stands up, hoisting himself on his good arm, his face is flushed bright red. Mrs. Grise stands, too, her hands gripping the edge of the table. *Don't they know what they're doing?* her head screams. *Don't they know there is already enough danger in the world?*

When Albert comes back outside carrying two backpacks, his father is bent over awkwardly, buckling Daniel into his car seat, and his mother has sat back down on the driveway with her work. Albert goes to kiss her and when she hugs him, her eyes are wet and won't meet his.

Later that evening, when Albert's father returns the children, Albert is very surprised to see his mother and Mrs. Grise standing in Albert's front yard. For so long now, he has never seen the neighbor leave her house. The two women stand looking up into the high branches of the tall oak in Albert's yard. The Grises' expandable aluminum ladder is propped against the tree.

"Don't pick it up," Mrs. Grise says. "I've always heard you should never touch one."

Albert sees the baby bird lying on the ground. It appears almost naked with a soft downy fuzz instead of feathers, its eyes still shut. He blinks: such a small thing. There is a breeze, no more than a breath, and Albert sees for an instant how little difference it would make to the world if the bird weren't there.

"I don't think that's true," Albert's mother answers Mrs. Grise. "Most birds have a poor sense of smell." She puts her hands on her hips, stares confidently up the ladder. "The first thing we have to do is find the nest it fell from."

Albert's mother begins to climb, the neat cuffs on her blue jeans rising above them.

There is a giggly rustling of leaves, and in a moment a disembodied voice calls down, "There's nothing here."

Albert watches Daniel bend down to explore the bird. His t-shirt slides up, exposing several inches of his baby white back and the elastic band of Pooh Bear briefs. His small fingers reach to touch.

"No!" Albert says. "Let Mommy do it."

Mrs. Grise stands with her fingers clenched inside her skirt pockets. She wants to help, she really does, but doesn't know exactly what to do. She came only because Kate knocked on her door, crying. But now that she is here, outside where she can feel the wind blow, she realizes she is afraid to do anything these days, afraid of the terrible, terrible damage one small movement can cause.

But the nestling begs for food, opening its mouth wide. Albert's mother climbs back down the ladder. "A margarine tub," she says.

In her mind's eye, Mrs. Grise pictures the Rubbermaid squares and circles, glass jelly jars and plastic margarine containers stacked unused in a lower cabinet in her kitchen. But before she can answer, Albert's mother has loped away from them toward the screen door. Seconds later, she is back holding forth a shiny white plastic margarine tub.

Albert, Angela, and Daniel collect leaves and fill the tub to just below the rim. Albert's mother kneels down to pick up the bird but then leans back on her heels to reconsider. "I don't think I can do it," she says, amazed.

Mrs. Grise thinks she can hear a soft coo. She bends closer to the bird, next to her neighbor. Their knees touch. Her own breaths sound uncomfortably loud and harsh to her ears, and the hands she reaches forward look unused and unfamiliar. She clenches her jaw; she does not want to cry in front of Albert. Then slowly, very slowly, she cups her hands around the tiny body, careful not to squeeze.

Inside Kate's kitchen, Mrs. Grise picks up bits of Daniel's baby cereal with a pair of tweezers. This time when the bird opens its beak, she is ready and puts a small bit of food way into the back of its mouth.

"It'll need to be kept warm," she says.

Albert finds a heating pad in the linen closet upstairs and together they wrap a towel around the pad and set the margarine tub carefully on top, setting on low.

Albert's mother invites Mrs. Grise to stay for a cup of coffee, and they sit at the kitchen table talking while the children run back outside to play. The sky is rippled with pink streaks but there is a dark gray cloud in the west.

"My father loved birds," Kate says.

Kate's father was a perfect man; Mrs. Grise has heard her say so many times. He died when Kate was 19, just four years older than Mrs. Grise's son was when she drove through the stop sign. Kate's father didn't die because of anything anyone did wrong, though. He just died. Of a heart attack, while playing golf. He was the love of Kate's mother's life: a smart man, a handsome man, a perfect man.

Through the window, Mrs. Grise sees her husband's car pulling into their driveway. They had had a fight the morning of the accident; she had left the house in a huff to drive their son to school. Whose fault was it then, and did it matter?

Watching her husband climb out of his car now, she is pleased to think how surprised he will be to see her visiting at the neighbors'. When he asks her why, she will tell him how Kate came to her door, crying about the fallen baby bird she'd found. Crying.

Now, sitting at Kate's table, remembering earlier visits there as though a light has suddenly been shone on them, she listens to her neighbor talk a little longer, then rests her hand briefly on top of Kate's. And then she goes home.

It is dark and shadowy inside her son's room, its sloped ceiling low and covered with purple paisley wallpaper. Heavy Roman shades of matching fabric cover the two windows. The room is just as Mr. and Mrs. Grise left it a year ago. Their son's high school notebook jammed with papers sprawls on his desk. Brown paper-covered textbooks perch in an uneven tower. There are blue-striped pajamas that had been unceremoniously dropped on the floor that horrible morning, one pair of Nikes rejected in favor of another that had been ripped from his mashed feet with the impact of the other car.

While her husband sits on the bed with his head in his hands, Mrs. Grise stares at the shoes, picking one up gingerly by the heel. She holds it to her nose. She sniffs deeply and then again and then again. She sits on the edge of the bed next to her husband for a long time, eyes closed, shoe to her nose, tears falling.

In a while, he leaves without speaking. The globe sits in its mahogany cradle; the line circling the equator is thick blue. There are raised bumps running through the center of Australia and along the west coast of South America. The Pacific Ocean appears in graded shades of blue. Mrs. Grise reaches to touch the coast of California and the globe suddenly illuminates. She turns, knowing she will be heartbroken if no one else is there to see. But Mr. Grise is walking back into the room, already nodding, a stack of storage bags in his hands.

Albert is jumping on the trampoline when he feels the unexpected gust of wind. Now, suddenly, the sky is completely dark, and he knows it will soon rain. Higher and higher he bounces above the blue ocean that lies below him. He tries to imagine how high the waves might rise in California.

The finished grill, with its fine red lid, stands at the edge of the driveway. Beyond it, through the neighbors' kitchen windows, he can see Mrs. Grise leaning against Mr. Grise, her head on his shoulder, Mr. Grise patting her back over and over again.

Behind his own window, he sees his mother sitting at the kitchen table, hands wrapped tightly around a cup. She has not cleared their dinner dishes.

Daniel and Angela run past him in the grass, and each of their faces are the shape of a heart.

He knows El Niño is coming for all of them. Bounce high, the sky is dark. Another gust of wind, bounce high. There are no spotters here, and it is such a small circle of blue below.

IN HERAKLION

On Crete, light pours down with a liquid clarity; every color is luminous, every form bold. *This* is why Grace has decided to come here where the sunlight is both harsh and luxuriant, warming the rough-hewn landscape and putting everything sharply into focus.

Though right now she sits in the dark cab of a pick-up truck, following a shadowy and unfamiliar road that, with luck, winds toward Heraklion.

Because the back of the truck is filled with watermelons, Grace, Hallie, her friend of many years, and the native driver all ride together in the front.

Grace sits in the middle. She regrets her habit of insistent, blind politeness. Her legs are longer than Hallie's, her arm now sticky from the driver's sweat. She looks at him again from the corner of one eye and sees a small, wiry Greek, surely a foot shorter than either woman. His t-shirt has moon-shaped stains at each armpit and Grace can feel his muscles ripple whenever he turns the steering wheel.

He had offered them a ride at Khania, at the dock where the small inter-island steamer came in. Grace wonders what he'd thought then, seeing the two middle-aged Americans standing at the quay, one already bronzed by the Mediterranean sun but the other, Grace, pale with graying red hair, in wrinkled linen and bronze earrings. Hallie wore a bandanna and had the sleeves of her peasant blouse rolled up, a large ivory bangle on one wrist. Grace spotted Hallie first, standing with her hands on her hips, chin up, the way she had in college.

Grace was grateful Hallie had been there to meet her, just as she'd promised in the letter. They hugged then Hallie lifted her finger as though hailing a cab.

"I hitched here," she explained. "Takis' bus broke down. Again. But this man will get us home."

The t-shirted man had already started lifting Grace's suitcases into the back of his truck.

"So you left Jay to do the deed himself?" Hallie asked almost immediately after the driver started his truck. "You really think he'll tell his wife this time? You sure?"

Grace wasn't sure at all. She'd left Jay that morning, taking a week's vacation from work, because she thought it might give Jay more room with what had been his own decision. Though she didn't see how he could really imagine any such freedom, after their two intense years together, all those afternoons of peeled clothes dropped on the floor in her apartment as they rushed to get their hands on each other.

The moment the door pulled shut on the plane's pressurized cabin, she had wanted off. The vacation had been a mistake. But it was too late; the plane had already taxied down the runway. Jay was lost in the crowd at LaGuardia. Still, she had reassured herself, she could call him, just as soon as she reached the place Hallie was staying this summer.

"Hotel, fuck?" the driver asks.

Grace's hand shoots out to touch her friend's hip.

The driver smiles and tells them in broken English about his wife of six months, full and round with her pregnancy. He points back toward the melons.

The women look at each other.

"Let's sing," Grace says. "It's the only way to keep him out of our lives." They begin with *South Pacific*, the melons knocking hollowly in rhythm.

The one condition of their ride from the dock back to Heraklion had been that they stop to pick up the watermelons. So Grace's first sight of the coast and its mist-covered plains of olive trees came from a watermelon patch high above the sea. Everything seemed at such a distance below her—the peninsulas of chiseled rock, islands torn from mountains, everything stretching her view.

At the watermelon patch, they watched men in white shirts and black vests toss the green fruits from hand to hand. Once they tried to help but the melon slipped from their fingers.

Their driver laughed, winking, but the other men only frowned as their hard work broke into a rose mush in the Americans' clumsy hands.

Back on the road, Hallie pinches Grace fiercely and points at the driver, whose eyelids hang heavy and head nods perilously close to the steering wheel.

"Here!" Grace yells to wake him. The driver's head snaps back, his boot crashing down on the brake. She reaches for the door and both women scramble down to the road, throwing their backpacks and purses in front of them. Hallie climbs up to retrieve Grace's suitcase then they wave to the driver, say nonsense words in English.

The driver looks confused. "Hotel?" he says, squinting into the darkness.

"Just like some men," Grace says to Hallie. "Not to recognize rejection when it happens." They run a few steps down the road, giggling.

The truck starts to pull past them, the tops of the melons now glinting in the moonlight. Through the open window the driver says, "Heraklion, *theo*, two, miles. *Poli cone da.* Not far." Then he disappears down the road.

It's impossible for Grace to read her watch in the dark. She pirouettes, stretching her hands high above her head. All around them are tall oaks.

"Home to some dryads, maybe," Hallie says then tells Grace the legend of these nymphs, the beautiful, shy ladies of the forests. If a tree dies at the hand of a human, Hallie tells her, the dryad dies with it and revenge from the gods is swift.

"Well," Grace says. She wonders if Hallie is trying to tell her something else, something about men hurting women, something about Jay. But she doesn't want to think about it now.

"Well," she repeats, facing the one bright spot in the darkness that is Hallie's white blouse. "We got rid of the horny driver at least."

"Takis is a mother hen," Hallie says. "He'll be mad at me if I don't have you home soon."

Takis and his wife Sophie are hosting Hallie for the summer as she works on a dig at Mochlos.

"What's that?" Hallie sounds nervous. She turns and points behind them.

Grace's first instinct is not to look where she is pointing. Just as her instinct has been not to imagine what might replace afternoon visits and evening loneliness, phone calls received but rarely placed, that careful timing of natural urges. She hadn't once asked Jay to marry her, not ever. It was his idea. Sometimes this possibility excites her. Sometimes she is fearful of breaking the spell.

She peers down the dark road. If it were daytime, she knows, she would probably see white-washed houses through the trees, with poppy-tiled roofs and window baskets heavy with herbs. But now, everything is hidden in darkness.

Then she sees three small, bright orange sparks. Of fire? Small but growing larger even as she watches.

"Cigarettes," she says.

She grabs Hallie's arm and pulls her in the direction the driver had pointed them. They walk quickly, holding hands. Once, Grace looks back to see more clearly what is following them. The tips of the cigarettes are still there, but now she can also hear deep voices.

The men were just out for a smoke probably, no source of danger to them. Still, she realizes, she couldn't communicate with anyone here if they really needed help. This, combined with the unfamiliar road and late hour, gives Grace a sharp pain near her heart, a longing even for that earlier irresolution she had left back home.

Shortly after they'd met at a party Grace catered, Jay called to ask her to lunch. It was his wife who'd asked for her card but Jay slipped it into his pocket.

It surprised Grace that she accepted the invitation. She knew something would happen. It was almost like she dared it to. A few days after lunch, Jay was at her door with a copy of Saul Brodsky poems in hand, "A friend of the czar, sorrow, am I," he read. But a few hours later, he left in a fury, telling her he shouldn't have done this, he loved his wife. He didn't say so but she could tell he blamed her, Grace. At times, Grace thinks she'd been handled as unthinkingly as she and Hallie tried to toss that melon. Sampled, savored, spit out until the next appetite.

After what seems a long time, Grace and Hallie see lights ahead of them. Heraklion. The cigarettes and men's voices have disappeared behind them and they walk, relieved, into the neon-lit square. Loudspeakers are playing and a parade of Cretan youth, girls in flowery skirts, moustached young men in black shirts, pace restlessly across the square.

"That's it. There's Takis' hotel," Hallie says, pointing to a white stucco inn on one side of the square.

Lamplight pours from its windows. Under the eucalyptus trees in front, two old women in black dresses turn a pig on a spit.

As Hallie and Grace approach, a man rushes out the front door of the inn, his white hair standing almost upright. Despite the heat, he's wearing a wool suit and neatly buttoned vest.

Blue eyes sparkling behind black-framed glasses, he shepherds the women into the lobby.

"Ten," he says loudly, pointing at a gold pocket watch he pulls on a chain from his vest. "*Ti bora,*" he demands of Hallie. "*What time is it?*"

"Don't mind him," Hallie says to Grace while Takis shouts. "He cares too much. Now he can worry about you, too." She pats the innkeeper on his arm then looks around the room.

"Where's Sophie?" she asks.

"*Ecki para.* Over there." Takis points to a door at the back of the lobby. Grace notices small tables set around the room for other guests. A red-cheeked gentleman clips the end from a cigar. Two bearded young Americans play backgammon.

In the kitchen, Grace meets a stout woman with green eyes. Sophie wipes her hands on her apron before and after shaking Grace's hand then returns to her work, placing transparent sheets of dough in a large pan.

"That's beautiful," Grace says.

"*Arero!*" Hallie says to Sophie, laughing.

Hallie's quick translation makes Grace feel tired all of a sudden, and very alone.

She puts her hand out to touch Hallie, to ask where she might sleep. But just then Takis bursts into the kitchen, carrying a tray of jelly glasses filled with straw-colored wine.

"*Retsina*," he says, herding the women back to the lobby.

"That's Nikos, Takis and Sophie's son." Hallie points to a narrow-hipped young man who leans against a mantle over the stone fireplace. "Nikos will go to university in Canada next year."

Takis raises his glass to beckon his son to join them, then toasts each with a clink to their glass. "*Yamas*," he says. "To us."

Takis insists they sit at a table by the unlit fireplace. Others join them. By the raised voices and serious expressions, Grace wonders if the conversation that races around her may be about politics. She can't understand what any of them are saying. Once Nikos breaks out in English to say, "We give up our life before we give up our freedom." His mother, playing with amber worry beads in her lap, frowns at him.

Soon a woman comes in from the courtyard and begins to sing. Songs of melancholy regret and proud defiance. Songs that even in another language Grace recognizes as love songs. She feels a hand on her knee, slipping under the hem of her sundress. When she looks at Nikos sitting next to her, he stares back into her eyes but says nothing.

Grace shivers. The touch has reminded her of Jay. No one else has touched her for two years. Everything has hung in limbo, neither here nor there, as she resisted overtures from other men. When Jay said he would leave his wife, it caught her off guard. Maybe, she thinks, the little she had had in their arrangement had been enough.

She shakes the hand off her knee.

Men, alone or in twos and threes, begin to dance. Young men, old men whirl and dip in their dancing. They are graceful, exotic. Even Takis and Nikos dance arm in arm.

When she can no longer keep her eyes open, Grace stands to leave. Hallie takes her to her room upstairs. The room is small, with sun-faded wallpaper, an iron bed, and a flowered porcelain washbasin sitting on a nightstand near the bed.

"The bathtub's downstairs," Hallie explains. "Out back. There's a separate shed below Nikos' apartment. You can go in by yourself, but just know the door doesn't lock." She sits down on the bed.

"Takis is harmless, you know. Sometimes he does crazy things, like this stupid thing he does sometimes. Sometimes when I'm taking a bath, somebody will push a wad of crumpled paper through a hole that's in the door.

"Nothing's ever happened but that. I think Takis' playing games. I suppose it means he's looking at me, but I don't mind. It's harmless, I think."

"I suppose so," Grace says.

In the morning, Grace wakes feeling so hopeful and refreshed from the sea air blowing in her window that she decides not to call Jay after all. He has promised to send a wire. And Takis is already calling upstairs for them to get ready for the trip to Knossos.

He insists they leave early so they can get there ahead of the tourists.

"The traffic will be bad," Hallie translates, "And if we go now we can find parking close to the entrance. It is too hot to walk too far today, he says."

They find a parking space a block away and Takis hurries them to the entrance gate. He brushes the tour guides aside and, always ten steps ahead, leads them through the procession halls lined with frescoes, into the Throne Room, and past storerooms filled with unearthed bull statues, vases, and bare-breasted snake goddesses.

Hallie tells Grace that the palace was designed with such complexity that no one could find their way out. But Takis leads them deftly through the rooms, Hallie interpreting his rapid-fire explanations. Here, Theseus came to slay the Minotaur and later abandoned his prize, Ariadne, on his way through the islands. A guide at the palace climbs into one of the huge olive and wine jars to show them, See, how many thieves could hide here.

They stop at a taverna for lunch and eat fried red mullet, rice with raisins and nuts, honey and nut pastries like those Sophie had made. Once seated, Grace finds herself feeling exhausted again, tired of conversations she doesn't understand. As they eat, she blocks out even Hallie's comments in English and decides that when they get back to the inn she will spend the rest of the day alone.

On the drive home, Takis keeps one hand on the steering wheel and with the other points again and again, insisting we see and remember his island: the bone-white limestone, pink oleander, scattered groves of olives.

Late that afternoon she goes to the beach alone. She wants the still-bright sun to heal her and the gritty sand to rub the rough edges from her skin.

After a swim, she falls asleep on her towel. When she wakes, she sees a boy leaning against a log further down the shore. She hadn't seen him before, she was certain of that. Still, he looks like he's been sitting there forever, hardly moving, staring at the water.

"He's deaf and mute," Hallie says when Grace returns to the inn. "The son of a fisherman in town. He's awkward, almost pathologically shy. But when he goes out with his father to bring in the octopus, he's so beautifully sure-footed on their boat. As though he doesn't need to hear a single thing outside himself to keep his balance."

Grace tells Hallie she's going up for a bath, to wash the sand off before dinner. Once in her room, she sits by the window to cool herself and from there, spies a yellow envelope sticking out from under the washbasin. Takis must have put it there while she was gone. The paper is so light she can barely feel its weight in her hand.

In the message, dated that morning, Jay has written that nothing between them has changed, but he has decided he cannot tell his wife right now. He's afraid to let his wife go; her mother has taken ill; Nan is flying down to be with her. It is not a time to leave. But he is also afraid of—cannot even imagine—letting go of Grace. He asks Grace to come back early so they can talk. His arms and heart feel empty, the message says.

Grace feels uncomfortable. Something important has not been said. Jay has painted himself the injured one, insisting she be sympathetic to his frustrated desires. Surely, there is something more.

She drops the paper quickly back onto the nightstand and remembers that what she came up here for, one of the many things she needs right now, is a bath. She gathers up a towel and her toiletries and heads down the backstairs and outside. The bath house is ten yards from the main inn. Its door is unpainted oak, solid except for a circular opening at eye level. Inside, the room is bare except for a claw-footed enamel tub, a wooden bench, a tin bucket, and a water pump on the side wall.

She fills the bath slowly, carrying the bucket back and forth. When she is done, she tests the water with one finger, then drops her clothes in a heap on the floor. The tub is wide but uncomfortably short, too short to allow her to stretch to her full length.

She props her feet on the far rim then swirls the water over her stomach, thinking whether or not she wants to catch the next plane home.

She hears a soft brushing sound, then silence. She has to turn to look back toward the door she'd just come through. A crumpled ball of newsprint lies on the floor just inside the door. Sunlight pours through the small circle in the oak. Grace doesn't know whether to laugh or cry. If Nikos poked the paper through the hole, it's nothing more than the normal urgings of a young man straining to get away from his mother's apron strings, looking toward a new land and new life. But maybe it was Takis, as Hallie first thought, acting out some of those usually repressed desires in a way that really does no one any harm. Or do they?

Tears stream down Grace's cheeks. She turns away from the door, wondering if the crumpled paper contains a message for her, in a language she will at last be able to understand. Or even if, and this possibility reverberates across her mind, unable to balance itself between fear and hope, it had come slyly, firmly, from one of the other men.

LAMBADA

Corkie Lang was surprised that Naomi Berriman had hired a biracial couple to dance the lambada at her husband Bart's sixtieth birthday party. The young woman's striking red hair swung hypnotically over her bare back as she moved. Her partner, his black face conspicuous in the all-white crowd gathered in the courtyard of an elegant DC townhouse, wore an open collared shirt, tight black pants, and pointy-toed shoes. The man bent his knees so the smaller woman's groin wedged easily into his in a perfect and natural rhythm.

Most of the guests seemed amused, except for Naomi's father, Max. Max was a marketing executive, not much older than his son-in-law. He'd recently had heart surgery, Max told Corkie, that had caused a partial loss of memory as well as the loss of a client of three decades' standing, a major shoe retailer. Corkie knew that Max had picked her out of the crowd as a willing audience, one of the few people there who would take the time to listen to him. She also knew, from experience with her own businessman father, that he wanted her to see through his slight stutter and occasional memory lapse to the very articulate, successful man he had once been.

From the small table where the two of them sat, Corkie could watch the other guests. Mostly lawyers from Bart's firm and their spouses. Mostly rich and still successful. At least the lawyers were. Sometimes, one would laugh nervously at a particularly sexy move the dancers made, as though it reminded them of something they'd somehow misplaced or forgotten along the way.

Part of Corkie wanted to just sit there with Max, but finally she excused herself to go find her husband, Wray. She'd thrown Wray a fortieth birthday party just three months earlier. Most of their guests had been the same.

For that party, Corkie had asked Heidelberg Bakery to decorate a large sheet cake with a photo of her husband superimposed on the white frosting. The baker used a computer to copy the photo onto the cake, with a technique he had explained carefully to Corkie when she first placed her order. Yet when people at the party asked, she couldn't remember how it was done. All she knew was that she had given the baker, a stout man with stubble on his chin, a 4x6 color photo of Wray. The photo was ten years old, taken on their honeymoon in Bermuda. In it, Wray stood in front of a coral hibiscus, beaming delightedly into the camera. He had on a subtly-patterned gray sports jacket, his first expensive "non-work" clothing purchase; a white shirt; blue, gray and taupe tie; and clear-rimmed glasses just like the ones he wore now. From the front, Corkie had decided, Wray didn't look much different in that old photo than he did now. It was just at the back of his head, where his hair had begun to thin, that anyone would notice a difference. And probably no one would notice anyway, other than Corkie and her mother-in-law.

Wray handed her a flute glass. "Mumms. Try some."

She took a quick sip.

"Having fun?" He had to shout above the music but just then the dancers stopped and the courtyard grew quiet.

The dancers stood there, their sweat gleaming in the pink glow of outdoor lights. The woman waved a too-thin arm at Bart, who looked uncomfortable, and pulled him into the circular space the crowd had cleared around the dancers. The black man, both his shirt and pants stained with perspiration, simultaneously reached for Naomi.

Naomi was beautiful. Talented. Brave. Everything Corkie wanted to be but couldn't seem to manage. Naomi looked like a model, dressed like a model in knock-out clothes. Naomi was at least twenty years younger than Bart. Naomi was a painter. Her most recent show had life-size oil paintings of a castrated Christ and a photo of glistening worms piled on Naomi's shaved pubic area.

Earlier that evening, when Max asked Corkie if she'd seen his daughter's gallery show yet, he'd added, "If you haven't, don't go."

But Corkie had already gone; Wray had insisted. Naomi had hung a notice at the entrance to the gallery, a note from the artist, saying that she knew her New Orleans-born and bred parents, Max and Marian, wouldn't approve of what lay beyond the door. Max didn't and Marian, who had cooked the delicious jambalaya and shrimp étouffle for that night's party, remained discreet.

Corkie had liked part of the show a lot. She'd long admired Naomi's style and forthrightness, and she especially liked one huge triptych that showed a self-portrait of Naomi, naked and bleeding between her legs, cradling a baby's head.

She watched Naomi and Bart try to match the movements of their partners. Naomi was a natural. Bart was not.

She looked at her watch, wondering how soon they could leave. Unlike most of the other couples there, she and Wray had no reason to leave early. No babysitter waiting for them at home.

She felt sick just thinking about it. Three miscarriages and an ectopic. A tubal ligation that prevented future pregnancies.

She reached to touch Wray's wrist bone. The music was loud again and he had to bend close to hear her.

"I love you," she said and he smiled and nodded then looked back at the dancing.

Bart laughed when the red-haired woman thrust her pelvis into his. Naomi was still dancing wildly and well, just as Corkie had expected. She was beautiful with the kind of movie-star good looks that make everyone sit up and take notice. Her art did that, too, and Corkie was certain Naomi would die knowing she had said her stuff, announced to the world, "Look, here I am," and held their attention.

Corkie didn't think she'd done that.

While Naomi and Bart danced with their younger partners, Corkie looked to see Naomi's mother Marian standing by the glass door that led into the kitchen. The older woman wore a collarless blue silk dress with a single strand of pearls. Her hair was white and gently haloed by the fluorescent lights behind her. As Marian fingered her pearls, she seemed to slump, almost imperceptibly, as she watched the dancers. But then her eyes roamed to find Max and a smile played on her lips when she saw him still sitting at the far edge of the courtyard under a green and white striped umbrella, moodily fingering a drink.

Wray made a move towards the bar. "Want something?" he asked.

Corkie leaned against a high brick wall. A potted stand of maiden grass stood nearby. She had nudged one of her high heels off and was rubbing her foot on the quarry tile, hoping her nylon wouldn't run.

When Wray asked again, she looked up and shook her head no.

"I want a baby," she said, as if for the first time.

"Well, good," Wray answered. "We'll have one. Love and technology work wonders." He kissed her on the cheek and she inhaled his after shave, wishing they were home in bed making love.

"We'll see what the doctor says tomorrow morning," he said then turned to make his way across the courtyard. She lost sight of him in the crowd but in a few minutes, he was back, holding a Campari and soda.

"Don't drink too much of that, you'll slow the sperm." It was Lew Slade, another of Wray and Bart's partners at the firm.

Corkie looked down to see a run had snaked up her hose. Goddamn it, she thought. Goddamn *you*, Wray. Nothing's sacred.

Lew leaned forward to plant a wet kiss on Corkie's cheek. She placed her hands on his shoulders to keep him at bay.

Lew was one of Wray's classmates from law school, never a real friend but one who professed to be. He hadn't made the cut that trying time when the firm's compensation committee voted whether or not to increase a partner's share of the profits. It was a slap in the face, a turn about from when they'd agreed Lew could go on 80% pay in order to stay home one day a week with his new baby. The firm's P.R. department had even circulated a photo of Lew and his daughter that made it to the front page of the Business Section of the *Post*, "*Area Companies Meet Demands of New Era in Fatherhood.*"

Tonight Lew was drunk.

"You're a good one to talk about watching the liquor," Wray said. Corkie could tell he was joking, but she wasn't sure Lew could.

Lew grabbed Wray's elbow and twisted it in a tight wrestling hold. Their jackets twisted together too, flipping open to reveal neutral linings, then hung straight and separate again.

Lew relaxed his hold. "Hey, look, partner. My only concern is for the wellbeing of this firm. Goddamn megalith that it has become.

Believe that? Sperm, brain cells, protozoa, I could give a damn. Because
believe me, at this age, it's all breaking down anyway."

Wray laughed nervously, sputtering the Campari he'd just
swallowed onto his shirtfront. He pulled a handkerchief from his back
pocket to wipe himself off then looked up at Corkie.

"I'm sorry," he said. She knew he wasn't talking about the shirt.

Lew turned away from them, weaving his way toward a blond
woman in a short leather skirt who sat perched on a counter inside the
kitchen. Marian was nowhere to be seen. Corkie watched Lew reach
one hand jerkily toward the counter, the other landed on the woman's
knee.

"You told him about our appointment tomorrow," she said. She
couldn't look at him. "You son of a bitch."

Corkie was shy, a real introvert. Her score on Myers-Briggs had
almost gone off the chart, and one of many reasons she'd married Wray,
was his easy way with other people. He seemed able to bring the world
to her, giving her access to it in a way she would never have had without
him. He liked talking with people, and they with him, and she basked
in the reflected glory of his friendships. But sometimes, too, they grated.
There would be too many intrusions, unwelcome demands. And nothing
was sacred between just the two of them. Every decision they made
was announced and discussed with others. Sometimes she just wanted
him to stop talking to everyone else but her. Sometimes she wanted to
leave all those lawyers Wray loved to have nearby. But she grew fearful
whenever she pictured the isolating cocoon she would most certainly
weave about herself in a life without him.

The appointment tomorrow was to start their second attempt at
in vitro. The first attempt had been unsuccessful. For a few months,
Corkie lost all desire to get pregnant. Then, right around Wray's birthday,
something had changed. Looking at Wray's face on the birthday cake,
remembering how much she loved him, she worried she'd blown the
whole thing. They should have a family. Sometimes she fantasized their
home filled with kids. But by now she knew it was the number of different
fantasies she entertained that made any particular one hard to obtain.

The doctor had warned her that the chance of a successful

fertilization was slim. Already low, the odds went down dramatically for women over forty.

"It's not like you just fall off a cliff," he'd laughed, because this had nothing really to do with him. "Thirty-nine, forty-one, there's no one point when the odds drop," he continued, more seriously now. "It's just that the chances for you aren't going to be even as good as they were five years ago." He hesitated. "Though the process itself is vastly improved. The odds have gone up a lot. And you'll find it much easier this time around, believe me."

Wray was tugging at her arm. "Where are you, Corkie? Look, I said I'm sorry. I made a mistake telling Lew. I'm excited about it, that's all."

There were shadows under his eyes, tell-tale signs of overwork and stress. Sometimes in bed she'd look at the delicate skin there, remembering his tenderness beneath the bluster.

He smiled. "It'll work, pumpkin. Don't worry."

Corkie smiled, too, at his inadvertent use of the name her father had called her when she was little.

"It's okay," she said and tried very hard to imagine it was.

Just then there was a commotion at the far end of the courtyard. Something—a chair?—fell over and several men moved quickly towards the noise. A striped umbrella blocked Corkie's view. She pulled off her other shoe and stood on tiptoe, leaning her weight against Wray's shoulder and peering around peoples' heads, until she saw that what the men had moved towards was Max.

His head had fallen onto the table as though he had tired of drinking, tired of straining to recreate his past, and had slumped unconcernedly on his face to nap. But he wasn't lifting his head, even though someone was grabbing his shoulder and shouting his name. A small crowd had gathered around the table to give him the attention he so recently craved, but Max wasn't buying.

"What happened?" Wray asked.

"It's Naomi's father. I think he's had a heart attack."

"My God." Then, "We've got to get an ambulance."

As Wray moved toward the house, Corkie watched one of the guests wave his arms and the group gathered around the table pushed back, clearing an open space the way they had done for the dancers. A woman in a pink dress stood immobile, biting her lip, until someone else grabbed her and pulled her away.

Bart was one of the two men who remained at the table. He gently lifted Max's head, cradling it in one arm while his free hand pulled up one of his father-in-law's eyelids.

He pressed his ear to Max's nostrils and then his chest, then pulled a blue placemat from the far side of the table and laid Max's head gently back down on it. Bart tugged Max's tie loose and opened the top button of his shirt. He looked up, frightened, when Marian's voice, clear and lovely, filled the improbably still air of the courtyard. Corkie turned to see Marian in her blue dress beside the sliding glass door.

"What's going on out there?" she called out. "Where are the dancers?"

A man Corkie didn't recognize whispered into the white hair covering Marian's ear. Corkie watched the woman's face crumple. The man took hold of Marian's elbow and led her toward Max.

Wray was back. "Where's Naomi?" he asked.

"I don't know," Corkie answered, realizing how long it had been since she'd seen their hostess. "I don't know where she is."

"Find her." Wray started walking over to where Bart still stood at the table with Max. Marian was bending over her husband. Corkie couldn't see her face.

Quickly, Corkie shoved her shoes behind the potted maiden grass and headed toward the kitchen. As she walked through the door, she saw the blond woman still sitting on the counter, peering into a compact and applying lipstick to her lips. No one else was there, so Corkie continued into the den with its grand piano and up the white metal stairs that spiraled through the four floors of the townhouse. On the second level, tall canvasses leaned against the center pole of the stairwell and against one white wall. A huge chalk drawing stood propped against the wall, a woman's nude back, her arms raised high above curved shoulders, beseeching an invisible presence.

When she reached the third floor, Corkie heard something and cried out, "Naomi?" But it was only a woman stepping out of a bathroom.

She looked embarrassed, knowing there was no reason for her to be up here.

"Just had to see the rest of the house," she giggled.

"Have you seen Naomi?" Corkie asked.

"No. What's she up to now?"

She doesn't know, Corkie thought. Quickly, she hurried up another flight. Here a long hall was lined with some of Naomi's early canvasses, oil paintings that were mostly scenes from New Orleans: a glistening black-skinned woman with a blue bandanna, four men playing cards by the light of a gas lamp that seemed to flicker even as Corkie walked by.

There was one more half-level, where Naomi had her studio. In stockinged feet, Corkie climbed up to the closed door at the top of the stairs and pushed it open.

Two bodies lay on a futon on the floor. As soon as she saw them, Corkie knew she had somehow expected this. Naomi's torso gleamed while the man's arms and shoulders had taken on the dull sheen of black velvet. His face was hidden between her thighs, and Naomi was staring at Corkie.

"What in God's name do you want?"

For a moment, Corkie forgot what she'd come for. She stood transfixed; Naomi was so beautiful. She didn't want to say what she had to say, not to this woman, not ever. But finally she managed to whisper, "It's your father." She swallowed, finally remembering to cast her eyes down. "I think he's had a heart attack."

Then she looked up again to see Naomi push the man's head from between her legs. Naomi stood up, more vulnerable than Corkie could ever have imagined, and reached for a terrycloth robe that hung from a hook on the wall.

"Shouldn't you put on something else?" Corkie asked, knowing even as she said it how absurd this would sound.

"I don't give a damn what they think. Any of them," Naomi answered. She stepped over the dancer's body toward the door. The man remained where he lay on the mattress, his head propped on his arm. He smiled. Corkie started to smile back then stopped, turned, and ran back downstairs.

By the time she reached the street level, the ambulance had arrived. The siren had been turned off, but its red lights circled ominously, throwing splotches of color onto the houses nearby.

The front door stood ajar. The woman who'd been snooping upstairs stepped forward to open it even wider so the medics could wheel a stretcher through. When they came back a few minutes later, Max was lying on the stretcher, his eyes closed and a satisfied smile on his lips. Bart followed close behind, clutching Marian's hand. Naomi was nowhere to be seen.

Corkie spotted Wray following Bart and the medics up from the courtyard. Together they moved to a window at the front of the house to look out at the scene on the street.

When the medics reached the ambulance, they lifted the stretcher and started to push it inside. Bart had his arm around Marian's shoulder now. Corkie heard a noise then from the level above them and walked over to look up the staircase. She saw Naomi, her bathrobe loosely tied around her waist, standing by the large drawing of a woman's naked back. Corkie watched as Naomi pulled something from her pocket, then began to slash the canvas.

In silence, Naomi finished her task. Then she ran down the stairs, brushing past Corkie, as she headed out the door. She reached the stretcher just before it disappeared into the ambulance. Corkie could hear her sobbing, "Daddy, Daddy." Naomi had grabbed Max's hand from under the sheets. "Not now, Daddy. Not yet. I didn't know what you wanted. I didn't know you would go. Please, Daddy, don't go."

Corkie grabbed Wray's hand and held it tight. Naomi still held Max's, but one of the medics pried it loose. Surprised, she looked back toward the house, her eyes locking on Corkie's. Black streaks of mascara and kohl striped her cheeks.

"Wray," Corkie whispered. He slipped his arm around her waist. They watched the medics climb into the ambulance and drive away. Bart, Marian, and Naomi got into Bart's Jaguar parked at the curb. Corkie could hear Naomi's shrieks as the car moved away from them down the street.

After a moment, when the street had grown quiet and the few

neighbors who had ventured out returned to their homes, Corkie stepped back from the window. She removed Wray's hand from her waist, but followed him back downstairs to the courtyard.

A few guests still stood by the bar.

"Well, it's high time for one now. I'm sure you agree." Lew had his arm around the waist of the blond woman. She smiled up at him gratefully. He grabbed a bottle of Chivas from the bar, and the two of them disappeared into the house.

Wray reached for a bottle of champagne and two glasses.

"How do we turn the CD player off?" someone yelled from inside.

"Leave it," Wray said. "We'll get it later."

Corkie looked back to the table where Max had been and saw the lambada dancers sitting there now, listening to the music. The man had his black pants and white shirt back on, the red-haired girl had her chair pulled close to him and was smoking a cigarette. When the man saw Corkie, he jerked the cigarette from the girl's fingers. He pulled her up from her chair, then led his partner to the middle of the courtyard. They began to dance, slowly this time, one black arm wrapped tightly around the girl's thin waist.

Wray poured the champagne, gulped his down, and looked over at Corkie.

"Well?" he asked.

Corkie wasn't sure what to answer.

"She was afraid," she said.

"Who?"

"Naomi. She was afraid." Corkie thought about how Naomi had disappointed her, that what she'd thought was real wasn't.

Wray put his glass down and reached his arm around Corkie's waist then pulled her close to him. She could smell Campari on his breath, feel the wonderful warm solidity of his chest. She could stay in his arms forever, she thought. Just like this.

But she refused to look at him, looking up at the trees behind the bar instead, their leaves dark and tinged with purple at the top. The sky was clear. A breeze stirred the air. All of the guests had left but the lambada dancers still danced in the middle of the courtyard.

"Wait a minute," Corkie said, pulling off her hose, now hopelessly run.

When Wray took her into his arms, she stepped in her bare feet onto his shoes. They danced, his shoes moving only a little at first, and his arms keeping her pressed tightly against him. She saw a trickle of sweat run down the back of his neck and wiped it gently with one finger. For a moment they moved perfectly in rhythm.

"It isn't going to work, you know," Corkie said suddenly, stepping back onto the cold tile. "The in vitro, I mean. It isn't going to work."

Wray looked over at the other couple. His lips stayed closed but his feet kept moving.

THE GREAT DRAWING
BOARD OF THE SKY

Carolyn holds the doll's head under the faucet in her son's bathroom sink, wetting the stiff blond hairs until they darken and flatten. The clumps of hair are rooted in rows of holes that suddenly nauseate her with their heartless precision. There's ink on the cheek her thumb can't rub off.

She grabs Timmy's comb from the counter, tries to run it through the doll's hairs but she can't do that either, so she pats them down hard against the uncompromising plastic head. She is crying.

In Timmy's room, she opens a drawer filled with nightshirts and the Superman bodysuit she'd sewn him for Halloween, and finds a too-small red tartan pajama top into which she pushes the large doll, rolling up the sleeves and buttoning the top button so the gash in its neck won't show.

Timmy is in the small room where they keep the television. He can hear his mother crying. He pulls out the Civil War tape and sticks it in the VCR. He likes the music, the serious, grown-up voices—"We have shared the incommunicable experience of war." Most of all, he likes the black-and-white photographs, and the way he can see what death looks like in their comfortable, quiet flatness. He studies the men— their bandaged arms and legs and heads. He stares back into their eyes as they once looked into the photographer's lens, catching a quick image of his own face reflected in the screen. He sees the men sitting upright, posed for a picture, and lying flat on the battlefield. Both kinds of photographs are motionless, yet he knows that one reveals a different, more threatening stillness.

Behind Timmy's bed is the life-size papier-mâché statue of a woman soldier, wearing the cocoa and tan uniform of war that Carolyn made. She's a theatrical designer, maker of props, masks, marionette heads, and break-aways for the stage, and a sculptor of large-scale human forms.

Since Timmy's father left them last spring to return to Peru, she'd been filling the rooms with the presence of others. She wasn't unhappy he had gone. At least her statues didn't scream at her, call her obscene names and leave small bruises on her arms.

In the living room a row of old women dance, arms linked at the elbow, legs raised, toes pointed. A scarecrow in a striped shirt and nylon hose head sits at the table where they eat their meals, and a bus is parked next to the bathroom, a man poised to descend from its steps. And everywhere, stuck to the high ceilings far from reach, glow-in-the-dark stars and suns and moons. At night, they shine eerily green. She'd needed a ladder to put them up there when Timmy was four. Back then she often lay in bed with him at night to whisper stories, until Adan would walk in, chugging his chica beer and slurring his words.

As Timmy grew, she'd taught him how to read the evening sky, season by season. How to find the constellations and what to look for in each: the Horsehead nebula in Orion, brilliant Sirius, the white dwarf remains of a star that had exploded centuries before them.

"Take me up there, Mommy," he would whisper as they lay in bed on their backs. And she had told him about his birthday constellation, Scorpius, with bright red Antares at its heart and another star at the end of its great sweeping tail, like the sting button of a real scorpion.

One night, she told him the story of giant Orion, the hunter, who boasted that so great was his skill, he could kill all the animals on the face of the earth.

"Unh-unh-unh-unh-unh. Unh-unh-unh-unh-unh." Timmy made a sound like a machine gun that startled her.

"No," she said. "Orion didn't have a gun."

"I would have. Or a cannon. I'd blow them up!"

She turned to look at her son's beautiful profile—his dark hair, the soft curves of his cheek and nose. Sometimes when they talked late at night, she looked to him for clues to the universe, the way an astronomer might study a chart of the sky.

"Did he do it?"

"What?"

"Kill all the animals."

"No. Not in my story. A goddess named Gaea thought about what a sad place the world would be without its animals. So she sent a giant scorpion to sting Orion. And then the mighty hunter had to die."

"Pow! Got him. My bug saved the day." He reached over to hug her. "I love you, Mommy."

Every night, after the story, she would kiss him and ask him to bring her back a moon rock when he returned from his dreams.

Now Timmy is seven, and sometimes after she kisses him good night, he whispers, "Stupid." Tonight at dinner he told her to shut up when she asked him what happened at school, and she sent him to his room. She heard him in there, throwing the doll around. She was working in her studio and tried to ignore it. When he finally came out he whispered, "You stupid ass," and before she could stop herself, Carolyn swatted him. He screamed and punched her in the stomach. She grabbed him by both arms, hard, but when she saw the look on his face immediately let go.

When Timmy was two, they'd taken him to Chosica to see some of Adan's family. It was Easter time and in the cobblestone courtyard in front of their hotel, a large papier-mâché Judas had been hung from a small scaffolding. The thing fascinated Caroline—the way its colorful bits of paper seemed to shimmer with a life of their own.

The last night before flying home, Adan went drinking with his friends so Caroline kept Timmy in the hotel and stood at the window of their room while he slept, looking out at the stars and not recognizing them. A crowd gathered below her and she saw hundreds of lit candles then fireworks as the papier-mâché Judas was blown apart and candies and coins fell from him onto the ground. When Adan finally crawled into bed with her, he stunk of alcohol and perfume.

Back in New York, Adan spent less and less time in the apartment. She didn't mind when he travelled for work or worked late, though she hated worrying that he might be with another woman. But when he was gone, the apartment was quiet and once Timmy was asleep there were no other demands on her. She'd stay up til the early morning hours, refining her technique with paper mash, pressing it into Plaster of Paris molds and pasting strips of newspaper on fragile earthenware pots or forms of cardboard and wire. Each year on Timmy's birthday, she made a piñata then watched her creation's fulfillment come at its moment of destruction, just like the exploding Judas in the square. Once, when Timmy was two, he smashed one of her sculptures, thinking there was candy inside.

In the television room, Timmy turns down the volume on the VCR to find out if his mother has stopped crying. She has cried less since his father has gone, and he is happy not to hear his father screaming at them. He hears the lock on his bathroom door open, hears his mother's bare feet padding toward him. He pictures her in the hall: her beautiful blond hair, the small upright lines between her brows that let him know when she is angry. He has a photograph of her on his dresser, one taken before he was born. She stands on a beach in a man's raincoat, barefoot and smiling. Sometimes at night, after she has gone to her room, he slides the picture under his pillow. He touches it with his hand all night.

Now, he listens to see if she is going to stop at the room where he is or walk on down the long hall to her studio. He wants to go to her but doesn't know what to say. He could ask for a glass of cold water; that usually works. But he doesn't want to see her face until he is sure she has washed it, and there are no sign of her tears.

Carolyn leaves the bathroom and passes the closed door where Timmy is. *Let him watch TV*, she thinks. She had been working on a new piece, and she wants to get back to it—a female figure who will sit in on the small parties Carolyn sometimes gives in the loft now for other artists and gallery owners. In a few weeks, the statue will be ready to lift her glass with the guests.

She has already stuffed a large paper bag with crumpled newspaper, tying it in the middle for a waist and at the top for the neck. The arms and legs are made of rolls of paper. She has built up the anatomical detail carefully, pasting, folding, and wrapping strips of newspaper around the body, arms, and legs, modeling facial features from the mash. Five slender tubes of rolled paper with pieces of coat hanger inside make the fingers. When she is finished she will dress it in a bikini and sit it in a director's chair in the living room.

Carolyn rarely knows exactly what she will do before she does it. Even if she has some idea how the figure will turn out, she knows that somewhere along the line, changes will happen. As she works on her figures, she can see the rhythm and relationships between the parts of the body more clearly, and often she'll find that she has to abandon her original concept. The sculpture grows under her hand, always with its final form different from what it started out to be. She knows she must do this with Timmy as well but trusts the process less.

In school, Timmy is well-behaved. Sometimes when he gets nervous, he chews paper, ripping small triangles neatly off the corners and putting them in his mouth when the teacher's not watching. He never brings anyone home to play.

The windows in the living room of the loft are tall and wide and look down on Third Avenue. Sometimes he stands and presses his nose against the glass. One story below him, he can see the green and white striped awning of the fruit and vegetable stand. Once, after his father stopped coming home, he carried the statue of the man stepping down from the bus over to the window and fit himself under its arm. He imagined that if someone looked up they would see a happy family.

When he hears his mother's footsteps pass the closed door, Timmy slips out to go to his room. He sees what his mother has done with Buddy, picks up the doll from his bed, and hugs it. He carries Buddy down the hall and stands for a moment silently at the open door to her studio.

Inside, he sees his mother bent over in front of a figure, one he does not yet recognize. She is brushing clear liquid on the form. Timmy stands there, squeezing his doll tighter and tighter. Finally he says, "I'm sorry, Mommy."

Carolyn is afraid to turn to look at him. His abuse of the doll has upset her, revealed things she doesn't want to see. His anger must be at her, and somehow she must be responsible for putting it there.

"I think Buddy needs a doctor," she says quietly.

She turns but he's gone, running down the hall back to his room. Tears flood her eyes, and then miraculously he's back, smiling.

"I've got my tools, Mommy. I'll find his wound and make it better."

"Okay." She is afraid she is going to start crying again, and she knows how much he hates it when she cries.

The next day the teacher at school phones to tell Carolyn that Timmy got into a fight with one of the boys at school. Carolyn is so upset she cannot work all day. She feeds Timmy his dinner in silence and is surprised when he asks her to lie down with him at bedtime.

"Mommy," he says. "Will you read to me?"

She picks up a book from his nightstand and begins. "In the ancient Chinese Annals of the Bamboo Books are accounts of the birth of a line of emperors. All began as detached souls in the form of fiery light. Then as shooting stars, one by one, they entered a human embryo being carried by the various mothers of these emperors-to-be."

He falls asleep with one arm over her neck, the other holding the bandaged Buddy. It is a long time before she carefully slips from the bed and returns to her studio.

She stands in front of the figure she'd been working on before that morning's call. The spackle has dried, and she mixes powdered red pigment into white paint to get a flesh color. She dabs a bit on then opens the floor-to-ceiling casement windows to let in fresh air.

She hears a noise and looks out into the hall to see Timmy racing toward her on the kick scooter they store in the closet.

"Don't..." she starts to say, moving to keep him away from her work. He's coming towards her, fast. She considers jumping out of the way, watches in horror as he crashes into the seated, expressionless figure she's been working on.

"Stop it, Timmy, stop it. That's Mommy's. That's mine!"

She grabs him to stop him from doing more damage, but he pulls away and heads toward the kitchen. She runs after him. Timmy opens a drawer and pulls out a knife.

"Put that back, Timmy," she screams. "Now. Listen to me, Timmy. Put that back."

From down the hall she can hear the muted sounds of the television; ludicrously, she wants to remind him to turn it off. "We have felt, we still feel, the passion of life to its top..." *It's the Civil War tape again*, she realizes. "In our youths, our hearts were touched with fire."

Timmy runs across the hall into the open dining room and drives the knife into the neck of the scarecrow at their table. Nearly three month's work. Then, he's on to the row of old women. He punches in their stomachs, knocks them flat, their purpled legs fly comically in the air. Nauseated, Carolyn thinks she might faint. He runs to the bathroom, Carolyn right behind him. He rips down the statue of the man in the bus and falls, crying, on top of him.

Aghast, she inches toward him.

Triggered by her movement, he jumps up and slips past her to the scooter. He's headed back toward her studio.

"Timmy!" She sprints toward him just in time to see him, and his scooter, slip silently through the open windows.

"Timmy!"

Half-thinking she will follow him out the window, she runs

forward and leans out to see him, miraculously, lying on his back, unhurt, on the awning below. The scooter lies next to him.

"Momma," he says.

"Just wait there. Don't move."

She stares at him a moment longer, soaking in his presence.

"I'm coming down to get you, Timmy."

At the emergency room, the doctor tells her that Timmy is going to be fine. He's a lucky boy, he says, placing a gentle hand on Carolyn's back. He gives her the phone number for a therapist on Second Avenue. He's arranged an appointment for them both on Monday.

Back home and tucked in bed for the second time that night, Timmy asks her again to read to him until he falls asleep. She opens the library book to a random page, and reads out loud about the Sumerians, who believed the sky was a vast battlefield where gods and demons fought in deadly combat. There was one super-god, she tells Timmy, who ruled over all the lesser gods.

"He was called Anu," she says.

"What's that mean?"

"'That which is above.'"

When Timmy falls asleep, she walks from room to room in the apartment, picking up the pieces of her destroyed art and throwing them away. She touches each piece tenderly. Before she closes the windows, she searches the sky again, tracing with her mind's eye imaginary lines drawn between the hard points of reality that are stars, joining things that only seem to be completely separate and turning them into unbroken figures, constants in a changeable sky.

HINDSIGHT

The gossip that summer of 1970, spiraling like the sparklers Tom and Jason insisted on lighting as they stood on the Paludans' new deck, circled lazily but returned again and again to one bright focal point: Jessie.

I first met Jessie in 1963 in Lawrence, Kansas, at the Salad Bowl, an annual costume party in the park where you dressed as your favorite salad component. I used a hula hoop and brown fabric to turn myself into a wooden bowl; Jessie had papier-mâchéd old newspaper around her to become a clove of fresh garlic. When she saw me, she walked over, rubbed her hip against mine and laughed.

It turned out both our husbands taught at the University—my Jason in the History Department, Jessie's Tom in English. And we were both pregnant and lived in the same block on parallel streets, Indiana and Ohio. In Lawrence, all but nine of the states have a street named after them.

We grew big-bellied, sweeping vigor, hope, and our own bulky sexuality into every neighborhood gathering under full, gracefully swinging smocks. When the children were born, two for Jessie and Tom, three for Jason and me, fireworks took on new life. That summer in Lawrence in 1970, when Abbie Hoffman came through and said, "K.U. is a drag, fuck it, I'm going to Houston," they were better than ever.

Looking back now, I see that Fourth of July as a real turning point, a day that if I'd acted differently, my life might have taken another path. Jessie and I had known each other six years by then, years when we talked almost every day. That summer, a year after the unflappable Neil Armstrong fulfilled Kennedy's promise of bringing us the moon, the fireworks seemed more dazzling and full of promise to us than they ever had before.

"They must have some new technology," Jason said that night as we stood on the deck watching the sky. "Like laser beams that can slice metal or signal outer space."

Each fireworks display, like each rumor bandied about town that summer, would trail off into the black sky, into a close and weighted silence. Tom's niece was divorcing her husband to follow an aging rodeo star to Partridge, Kansas; the woman who ran the clothing store at 10th and Massachusetts had swallowed twenty Elavil and sideswiped the Chancellor's car with her Toyota Corolla. We weighed the possibilities, the seriousness of the crimes.

That night, just when the fireworks seemed finished for the year, the sky above Indiana Street was lit by another burst of light. Our children, caught stifling yawns, were once more alert and wide-eyed. Just one more, they cried, their eyes heavy-lidded. Just one more.

"That's it," Tom said, lifting Danni, his littlest girl, in his arms.

When Jessie and I first met at the Salad Bowl, Tom was teaching in the English department and writing a dissertation on Robinson Jeffers. By 1970, he'd quit the university and become a reporter for the *Journal World*. He'd never finished his dissertation.

"Be careful with her," Jessie said to him.

After he and Jason had walked or carried all five children to beds inside the house, they came back to the deck and began lighting more sparklers and waving them dangerously back and forth.

"Don't *do* that," Jessie said. "One stray spark could do us in."

"Maybe that'd be for the best," Tom said. "Just think of the insurance money."

Jessie narrowed her long-lashed eyes. She was sitting on the top railing of the deck, kneading her calves with her hands.

"She's beautiful, isn't she?" Jason whispered to me. I thought the answer to that was so obvious I didn't need to say it. Maybe I should have.

Jessie had long, straight black hair that hung nearly to her waist, with bangs cut straight above her brows. Her eyes looked like split pieces of rock quartz you could pick up off the ground at the quarry outside of town. They held that many shades of violet, that many startling facets of light and mood.

Even then I knew Tom didn't pay enough attention to her. When they first married, she'd told me, he'd read to her every night before falling asleep in bed. A favorite was "Cassandra," the Jeffers poem about the mad girl with the staring eyes.

She talked about Tom a lot as we sat on the deck almost every day that summer. We could talk for hours, as rapidly and cryptically as schoolgirls, but among all the amenities that had seemed so unattainable when we were in school. While the kids splashed in a blue-lined plastic pool or dug tunnels and baked molded pies in a leaking sandbox, we ate Oreo cookies and drank homemade lemonade from a tall, clear plastic pitcher, the pale circles of sliced fruit staring out at us like shocked eyes. The pitcher was one of Jessie's finds from Moon's Variety Store. She'd fill it early in the afternoon with lemonade or sometimes Kool-Aid for the kids. About five o'clock, she'd take the pitcher inside and add gin.

Liquor was one of the things that initially fueled town gossip. A secretary where I worked part-time cataloguing slides in the library said she'd heard Jessie had started going to an off-campus bar late at night and getting drunk. I told her then I didn't believe it.

But Jessie was definitely drunk that Fourth of July. She kept wrapping her beautiful black hair around her hand nervously. With flashing eyes, she touched Jason and me often as she talked to us, fingers lingering. She completely ignored Tom.

Egged on by her attention, Jason talked more than usual, going on about the book he was writing on William Quantrill, a Confederate guerrilla leader who led a raid on Lawrence in 1863.

"I saw *Dark Command*," he said, drawing a bright Q in the night air with his red sparkler.

That was the first I'd heard about him going to the movie. I looked to where he stood near Jessie with his leg up on a low railing, khaki pants hiked up to show tan and maroon striped socks.

"When did you go to the movies without me?" I asked. I was sitting in a butterfly chair near Jessie.

Jason said, "It's a movie about Quantrill."

"Isn't Audie Murphy in that other Quantrill movie, *Kansas Raiders*?" Tom asked.

"I think I've told you Tom has this thing for war movies," Jessie whispered to me. "Actually," she said more loudly, "the two things he really cares about are war and fucking. Deep down."

I heard Tom say "Bitch" as Jessie's glass slipped from her hand and shattered on the deck. "Although hardly," he continued. "Bitches go in heat, don't they? I haven't noticed that happening much lately."

Jessie bent down to pick up the shards of glass.

"Don't," she said.

But Tom picked up the box of sparklers from the railing and dumped them into the wet stain of spilled wine. "Here. Fire's out."

Nobody said a word.

Jason brought his foot down from the railing and moved to put his arm around Jessie. Tom turned to go inside the house. I sat frozen. I remember thinking I'd talk to Jessie about all this, comfort her, the next day when we were alone without the men. So the three of us sat on the deck without talking until Tom came back out about half an hour later and pulled Jessie onto his lap. The moon was the only bright spot in an otherwise pitch black sky.

Before that summer, I don't think Jessie or I had ever seriously considered any options outside our marriages. Everything we had worked so hard to acquire was too new, too exciting to relinquish. And there were so many other things to talk about.

It was a turbulent year on campus. The Student Union building burned; a law professor brought a suit against the government to test the constitutionality of the Vietnam War; and Harry Snyder got shot by an over-zealous security policeman while painting STRIKE on the front steps of Watson Library.

A group of women who called themselves the February Sisters took over a building the University owned on Louisiana Street, a building that bore a plaque commemorating the deaths of four men shot there during Quantrill's raid. The Sisters demanded a child care facility on campus for students' families, a separate Women's Studies program, and free gynecological care at Watkins Hospital.

Jessie was the first person to tell me when this happened. It was the day after the Fourth and we were standing in the front hall of her house. She was packing boxes to store in the basement. Cartons filled with ice skates, electric blankets, and cafeteria-tray sleds lined the dark oak floor.

"I know I'm late," she said. "Don't say a word about it. But better I do it now than never."

She had on a full gathered skirt of a gauzy blue; strands of gold shimmered through the fabric. Whenever she passed the open doorway, I could see the long line of her legs silhouetted by the sun.

She emptied one box onto the floor, dropping a badminton net into a tired heap of citronella candles in small tin buckets.

"Do you want to tell me anything?" I asked. She brushed her bangs back from her eyes and looked at me as though trying to decide.

"I don't know," she finally answered. "Bad times. You know. You get through them. I suppose that's what we'll do, too.

"You know, I've found another job," she continued. Jessie already worked part-time reading onto tapes for the blind. "I'm going to be typing a cookbook. There's a group of women: Nancy Abuza, Susan Cairns, Mary Ware. Some of them belong to the February Sisters."

"*This* isn't going to last," she said when the last box of winter things was down in the basement. I couldn't tell if she was waving her hand at the suddenly empty hall or at the kids who were now on top of the table digging into leftover cookie dough.

"Do you remember when Kennedy died and Mary McGrory said, 'We'll never laugh again?' And Moynihan said, 'We'll laugh again. It's just that we'll never be young again.'

"It's the passion I mean," she continued. "The way I can still hug them so close to me and plant kisses all over their bodies isn't going to last. And then what?"

And then somebody fell. One of the children, at first I couldn't tell which one, had fallen off the table. Jessie ran into the kitchen before me and bent under the claw-footed table. When she stood up holding the child, Danni, her blue gauze skirt was daubed with tiny spatters of bright red blood. She brushed back Danni's hair just as she had done her own, searched out the cut and, relieved to find how short and insignificant it was, laughed and kissed her daughter's forehead, cheek, nose, and both eyes. Her long black hair fell forward, covering both their faces.

When Jason told me he was going to push to finish his book on Quantrill by the end of the summer, I upped my hours cataloging slides. I was angry about it. I'd sit in a small room in Carruth Hall with the window blinds pulled down, the only light coming from a table-top slide viewer where I could line up six rows of slides. When I held the slides in my hand, they were shadowy and incomprehensible; when I set them down on the viewer they came to life: Olynthian houses, Middle Helladic pottery, silver drachmas.

I was angry at Jason because he was working so much, and I was angry at Jessie because I wasn't seeing very much of her either. The secretary in the Classical Archaeology Department told me she'd seen Jessie walking into the February Sisters' house on Louisiana Street a few times.

The cookbook came out in the middle of August. Jessie gave me a copy one afternoon when she finally asked me over to sunbathe on her deck.

She was wearing a black tank suit and lying on her stomach on a gold-and-white striped towel. The straps of her suit hung unsnapped.

"Lila told me she's seen you go into the house on Louisiana."

Jessie turned over on her back and hooded her eyes with her hands. I stared at her breasts, which were also tan. *That's the first time she's ever done that*, I thought.

"How's work?" she asked.

I turned my eyes away. "Okay."

She reached for a glass of lemonade from a tray. Drops of condensation dropped on to the flat plane of her stomach.

"Feels good," she said. "Do you remember that Robinson Jeffers' poem Tom always used to quote," she continued, "about 'truth as a fluid concept, poured from a barrel by vendors and politicians.' Now it seems all Tom does as a reporter is stick a mike in front of those same vendors and politicians and hang on every word they say. I'm sick of it."

"People change," I said.

"I want you to come with me tomorrow night. I want you to meet someone."

"Okay," I said. I moved over to the window box on the rail of the deck. Harvey Miller, Jessie's next door neighbor, was struggling to pull his old lawn mower out of his crowded garage. His mouth moved furiously.

Jessie sat up, pulled up her straps, and lit a cigarette. She took a long, sharp pull. Lying next to her was a piece of embroidery she'd been working on all summer. An ash fell on the canvas. When she rubbed it roughly with her hand, it left a cloudy smudge.

She sighed and dropped the still-red butt into the quarter-inch of lemonade pooled at the bottom of her glass.

"Do you ever think you might not know something really important about someone who was close to you? Like Jason telling us about Quantrill, that he lived this seemingly normal life in Lawrence under an assumed name, and then wham, went and started killing people."

I waited for her to say more.

She pointed her long toes and moved them in clockwise, then counterclockwise, circles.

"No matter how much I have," she waved toward the busy children in the backyard, "it isn't enough. It's not that every time I get something I want I don't want it anymore. Though that's close. It's more that there's always something else to want. Hunger."

She pushed her hair to the top of her head and stuck a tortoiseshell comb in it.

I didn't know how to answer.

The next day I heard another piece of gossip about her.

Otto Zingg, a friend who had borrowed Jason's guitar, brought it back to our house. Jason had run to get take-out from Don's Steak

House. He'd told me once that the men's room there had a Lucite toilet seat with Kennedy 50-cent pieces embedded in it. Even though Jason wasn't home, Otto planted himself on the big black recliner that sat between two tall speakers in our living room, flipping through *Screw*, the local underground paper, with one hand and rolling a Club cigarette paper with the other.

"No additives. So pure the fibers entwine when wet and leave no ash when burned," he said. "Want some?"

"No thanks." I wanted Otto to leave and Jason to get home so I could go meet Jessie at a bar she'd invited me to.

"You don't share your friend's vices?"

"What do you mean?"

"Jessie's building up quite a reputation in town. Ask her how many Yellow Sunshine tabs she has in her house right now."

He held a match to the end of the rolled paper.

It wasn't a surprise to me that Jessie smoked dope. We'd all done that and more, but after my kids were born, I'd stopped. I felt betrayed to learn from Otto that my best friend hadn't.

When I finally got to the Fiery Furnace to meet her, that was the first thing I asked. She said yes, she'd been smoking some grass, not doing anything more, and Otto Zingg didn't know what he was talking about with the Yellow Sunshine.

She was perched on a bar stool under a low cedar ceiling strung with rows of tiny, sparkling Christmas lights. She had on blue jeans and a sleeveless forest green blouse with stand-up collar. A local rock-and-roll group, Ann Brewer and the Flames, was making start-up noises in the back room.

When the outside door opened, I saw a young woman with long blond hair walk in wearing a brown-fringed vest. Jessie motioned her to come over.

"This is Mary Ware," Jessie said, putting one hand on my knee and one on Mary's wrist. I saw a rose tattooed there.

"Hi," Mary said. Her lips pulled back from her teeth when she grinned.

We made room for Mary to sit down on a stool next to us, and she ordered beer with tomato juice and a Flannagan, an egg on fried bread with bacon.

Jessie lit a cigarette and started humming along with the band. A few couples moved to the dance floor, some women danced there by themselves.

"What do you do?" Mary asked me.

"I have three children and work part-time on campus."

"Oh, right! Jessie told me about that."

"What about you?"

"I live on Louisiana Street. We've started a publishing collective, and it's actually bringing in enough to pay the rent."

A young man walked over and put his hand on Jessie's hair. "Wanna dance?"

"No," Mary answered for her.

We didn't say much the rest of the night, just listened to music and smoked cigarettes. I even bummed a few from Jessie.

Here's what happened next. Yes, I was jealous that night, and I knew something was going on, but what happened next still totally surprised me.

I was walking over to Jessie's, with Rachel and Adam and Hannah dragging their wagon and sandbox toys behind me, when I saw a red Mustang speed down Indiana Street and stop right in front of Jessie's house. The kids and I were about half a block away so even though the car windows were up, I could hear "Satisfaction" boom from the radio. When the motor turned off, it sputtered before it died. Then the door on the driver's side opened, and Mary Ware stepped out. She had her blond hair pulled back in a tight ponytail. She had on cut-off jeans with ragged threads hanging down very white legs.

I stood frozen, telling the kids to just wait, and watched Mary march up the front walk of Jessie and Tom's house and ring the doorbell. I saw the door open from the inside, saw Mary Ware walk into the darkness, then saw the door shut. I put Rachel back in the wagon and grabbed Adam and Hannah by the hands, and we went home.

The next day, Jessie told me she was leaving Tom. She said that Tom and she had had a fight over the weekend and that Tom had come home early yesterday afternoon to see if he could patch things up by taking Jessie skinny-dipping at the quarry. But Jessie was up at school reading a geography text onto a tape for the blind.

"I know where he found it," she said to me. Her eyes were wide open and shone dark purple. "Goddamn son of a bitch was going through my things. I never meant for him to see it." When she looked at me there were tears in her eyes.

I found out what she was talking about in bits and pieces. It seems that Mary Ware had written Jessie a letter in which she talked about Jessie's long legs and breasts. When Tom later told Jason his side of the story, he said that when he finished reading that letter he dropped the paper as though it had burned his hand.

"Anyway," Jessie explained, "he called her right then. The *nerve* of him. And the *nerve* of Mary to take him up on it." That's when I'd seen Mary walk up to their front door.

Jessie sat in the same black chair Otto had sat in. Her shoulders shook. I put my arm around her and made the kind of noises I made to my children when they stubbed a toe or cut themselves with a knife, when the worst part of their hurt was thinking that it would never go away.

Jessie asked me to help her move out of her house, and I did. She didn't take much, a few suitcases of clothes and some books. She said she and Mary were going to live in a group house and that she could earn enough to live on by getting another job on campus. The hardest part was knowing what to say to Danni and her older brother as they watched their Mom pack. She kept telling them she'd see them all the time every day, but I was crying so much I had to look away.

For days after I couldn't decide if I hurt for me, or Jessie, or the kids the most. I kept swinging back and forth and not finding a thing I could think about that wouldn't make me cry.

What Jessie did that summer made me dig my heels in deeper. I quit my job cataloguing slides and stayed close at home with my children. I let Jason work long hours and didn't complain.

Twice I visited Jessie at the group house where she had moved in with Mary and five other women who kept a macrobiotic diet and spelled out poems on a Ouija board. But it was hard to see her there, and I stopped going. She called me on the phone sometimes, and we'd talk for a long time, just like we used to, but after a while even that stopped.

During one of those calls she told me about the divorce proceedings Tom had started. She told me he was trying to keep her away from the kids, claiming that she was an unfit mother.

And he succeeded in doing that. Three years later, Jason and I attended his marriage to a 20-year-old cub reporter on the *Journal World*. Tom had grown a beard and read Jeffers' "The Beauty of Things" during the ceremony.

In two more years, when the cub reporter had a baby boy, Jason and I attended the christening, and under his arm Jason carried a signed copy of his published book on Quantrill. Much later, in 1978, Craig Stevens, who had graduated from K.U. and played Peter Gunn on TV, picked up the movie rights to the book.

Jason moved to Hollywood the next year, leaving Rachel, Adam, Hannah, and me in the house on Indiana Street.

So. Digging my heels in didn't do any good.

I finished raising my children by myself and now, all three of them have left Lawrence. I still work on campus, though full-time as a photography instructor, and I run a small business taking photographs of children. I haven't spoken to Jessie in twenty years.

Tonight, on the Fourth of July in the first year of a new decade, I sit on the front porch of my house looking up into the sky above the stadium, waiting for the show to begin.

I think how I could have done things differently.

I could have run into the house that night and shouted at Tom and told him to come back outside, to pay attention to the good woman he had and not lose her. I could have found out why Jason had gone to see *Dark Command* without me, but that somehow got lost in all the other things that started to happen. I could have stood up and hugged Jessie hard myself, instead of letting Jason do it, instead of thinking she would be there the next day to tell me whatever she had to say.

I heard a rumor that she and Mary Ware had left the group house and moved to California, but I don't know how life worked out for them.

What Jessie did in 1970 opened my eyes, but it took many years to understand what I saw. Jessie took a leap and risked everything. I saw her go for what she wanted and I saw myself sit there and hold on to my husband and children for dear life, and then lose them anyway.

As the first fireworks display brightens the dark night sky, I picture another porch where Jessie might even now be sitting, tucking her summer-tanned legs beneath her and playing with the ends of her black hair. She is smoking a cigarette and blowing the smoke from her mouth in a straight, clean line in front of her. Other women sit cross-legged on the railing or on pillows on the floor, some resting their fingers lightly on another's knee or shoulder. The tip of Jessie's cigarette burns brightly in this dark room.

As fireworks rise from the unseen stadium, I can see Jessie sitting on this porch in very clear detail, as though I have a sharp, new photograph of her in front of me. In this picture, I look into Jessie's eyes, trying to catch their light, looking for some sign that she found what she wanted. Looking for some sign that I was right not to follow her and never finding it.

With Jessie, I had counted on something that indeed I could not see, as we count on the moon when it is hidden from us in the bright of day. I had counted on friendship, Kennedy, and the collective, ardent hunger of the times to keep us together. Then one day, my eyes opened and nothing, not any of it, remained.

WHATEVER YOU WANT

This is how they found him: Hanging from a tall tree on the Monterey Peninsula. Above the rope his face had purpled, and his eyes ballooned wide open. He wore the red and green plaid flannel shirt she'd bought him at Susie Creamcheeze, blue Wranglers, and his favorite white leather tennis shoes. Some of his shit had leaked through his Wranglers and smeared his shoes, but most piled on the ground beneath him. The doctor said that happens, that everything opens up and lets loose. As if in rebuke.

Hank was found by a vacationing couple, out for a morning hike. Rita imagined it was sunny, the sky clear and mindless, a handful of clouds spattered like daubs of meringue. If you looked you could see all the way to the Pacific, or at least that part of it that snaked into the California coast. Pyramids of young cypress boats, small and insignificant, moved along in the water, and Hank was dead.

It happened near the end of 1969, the year the first artificial heart was implanted in a human and Abe Fortas, under fire for his ties to a stock manipulator, resigned from the Supreme Court. SALT talks began, Chappaquiddick happened, and Neil Armstrong walked on the moon.

These events touched Rita Booth's life lightly, in big, black headlines glimpsed under the lights of a 7-11 late at night. The world was in tumult, but this was overshadowed by more immediate happenings on campus, at the blue house on Ohio Street, in her heart.

When she got the phone call about Hank's death she was sitting on the floor of her rented room in Lawrence, Kansas. Sunshine Acid sat on a shelf in the closet next to the pillowcases her grandmother had cross-stitched in pink and green. Her friend, Ned Kehde, had brought the little square papers back a week earlier from his trip with Hank to California; Hank had decided to stay.

After she hung up, Rita sat holding her stomach and rocking back and forth. She looked at the flower pot, then shut the door to the closet so she couldn't see it. She'd get a drink, at a place she'd started hanging out just a few months before, the Catfish Bar and Grill. She figured she'd see people she knew, though it was a different, older crowd than she'd been used to.

The Catfish Bar and Grill had once been called the Rock Chalk after the outcroppings of limestone found all around Lawrence. It stood at the top of Mt. Oread, at the end of the campus on 12th Street. That spring, which would be Rita's last in Lawrence unless she decided to stay for graduate school, was the first time she'd ever hung out in a bar. It had grown addictive. She'd drink beer, Coors usually, until she felt comfortable enough to talk to people. If she drank just the right amount, she'd feel a very pleasant strength and sureness, like she was part of a crowd and easy among friends. Drugs had brought some of that safety but their magic was less predictable, and sometimes she'd wind up feeling more isolated and speechless than ever. Beer was better. She didn't mind repeated trips to the ladies room, where she could look into the mirror and see someone who was still somehow part of whatever conversation was going on at the table she'd just stumbled away from.

So after getting the call about Hank, Rita Booth went to the Catfish. She spent most of the evening there, drinking Coors and smoking Carltons, trying not to think. About eleven o'clock that night she was sitting across from Rick Hatcher, a TA she'd talked to, flirted with, several times before. He was married. That night, Rita didn't care.

She asked Rick what he remembered from the past year.

"What do I remember?" He ran his fingers through the thick blond curls that framed his face, and his blue eyes laughed.

"My Lai," he said. "Wondering about the guys who wouldn't do it. Wondering if I could say no like they did, or if I'd give in, *want* to do it. Walking on the moon."

"That's pretty good," she said, then added, "You know, I know you have a wife."

Rick studied the scratch marks on the table. Somebody had carved "The Love Machine" deep into the wood.

"Here's a good one," he said. "'You may visit our state but please don't stay.'"

Rita lit another cigarette. "Who would want to? Kansas is just a state to floorboard through."

"So sad you are," he said. "I wonder why." He poured beer into both their glasses. "That's why we need liquor by the drink. So people will want to stay." He took a sip and wiped the foam from his lip. "Sandy knows where I am."

Rita's stomach hurt. Her heart hurt. She tried to remember what she had believed in and why it now seemed all wrong. Hank had needed her and the others who lived in the blue house on Ohio. And they, with their tie-dyes and water pipes, their dramatic renouncing of middle-class lives, their late-night talks and penetrating, slowed-down stares, had not been enough to save him.

Rick's hand landed on her lap, and he grinned.

"Wait a sec. Don't despair yet. Kansas *does* have some pretty neat stuff. We're the geographic center of the continental U.S., for God's sake. We have small towns where they still have pancake races. And somewhere there's a living canvas wheat field that's shaped like Will Roger's head."

"Wow." She was impressed but didn't want him to have the last word. Not him. She looked across the room and for a minute thought she saw Hank, the way a man was standing, his short black beard. For a minute she expected him to turn around and grin at her. She was getting ready to smile back when the guy turned around. She swallowed and looked back at Rick, who burped loudly.

"There's Medicine Lodge," she said.

"Whassat?"

"Home of Carrie Nation."

"The anti-booze lady? Preserve me, honey." He laughed.

And then Rita started to tell him. "I have a friend," she said.

"Yes?" By now he'd moved over to her side of the table and put his head in her lap. He stared up at her with hurt eyes, so she ran her fingers through his hair.

"I had a friend named Hank." She took her fingers from his hair and looked away. "He was the first man I ever had a crush on here. At this college."

"Lucky boy."

"No."

Rita met Hank when he and Ned Kehde threw baloney onto the window of an apartment where she used to live. The apartment was on the second floor of one of the twin brick structures of Jayhawk Towers.

She was watching TV with her roommate Betsy when she heard the soft, puzzling slap. When she turned to look, she saw one, then quickly two, then three, mottled circles of lunchmeat plastered to the glass.

"That's gotta be Ned." Betsy's laugh had helped make her a national Miss Teen finalist from South Dakota. Now an ex-sorority girl, she'd started hanging out with Ned Kehde and a few other lapsed sorority girls.

When Ned came into the apartment he brought Hank with him, and right away Rita liked Hank's eyes and goofy grin that shone from his black beard and the bouncy tennis shoes that made it look like every step he took in them was fun.

Ned brought grass. Rita had never tried it before. She sat on the floor next to Hank, their knees touching, and it felt like an electrical charge. He passed the joint to her. Ned had opened the baggie to pull out a roach clip when Hank said, "Feel good?"

"Mmm-hhh." She wanted to climb into his lap, wrap her legs around him, kiss his mouth inside the beard.

Betsy got up and put something on the stereo. Spirit. Ned rolled another joint. After they shared it, Rita threw off her glasses.

"I don't need these!" The glasses landed on the couch. Betsy crawled over on her knees to get them, giggling, but when she tried to hand them back, Rita refused.

She couldn't stop laughing.

What a silly apartment. For the first time in her life, she had seen the limits of the place where she lived, the sickening mustard-and-brown shag carpet that ran through the rooms, plastic covers on cream lamp shades, the Mediterranean dining set and wood-grained laminate cabinets in the kitchen.

"This has gotta go," she said and stood up to pull out the tall bare branches Betsy had stuck in a basket and decorated with a flowered bikini and sun hat.

Hank moved to the couch. Rita followed him.

Ned Kehde said, "Rabbit."

"What?" Rita said. She knew he was talking to her.

"That's what you are," Ned said. "Scared rabbit."

That hurt her feelings, though she knew it was true. Suddenly she didn't feel so great. She found her glasses where they'd fallen through the cushions on the couch and put them back on.

"Hey," Hank said. "It's okay. It's not so terrible to be a rabbit."

She looked to see if he was kidding.

"Listen," he said, putting his hand on her knee. "There's a new movie just opened down at the Varsity. *Easy Rider.* Wanna go see it with me Friday?"

"Sure," she said, straightening up. She felt like her smile was too big for her face.

Ned stood up. "Lovebirds. Rabbits. We gotta go."

Rita looked toward the window. The sky was black, the courtyard covered in shadows.

"How do we get out of here?" Hank asked.

"Come on," Betsy said, giggling again. "We'll show you."

Hank opened the door to the brick-lined hallway.

"This way." Betsy pushed easily between them, ran down the hall, then stood pointing.

"The elevator. *Sirs.*"

Ned Kehde followed her and pressed *Down* with his forehead. He stayed that way.

"Not me," Hank said. Rita noticed a short, gray scar above his left eyebrow. "There's gotta be a better way." He bounced up and down in his shoes.

"There's stairs," she suggested hopefully.

"Great. Show me."

She took his hand and walked him to the other end of the hall where a red bulb glowed. She pointed to the window in the top of the door to show him the stairwell.

Hank opened the door, then turned to press his face against the glass. His lips flattened, then he pulled away and mouthed, "See you."

That was the first time falling in love made Rita laugh.

Rick Thatcher squeezed her hand.

She squeezed back half-heartedly.

"Can I come visit you?" he asked.

She looked to see if the guy who looked like Hank was still at the bar; he wasn't.

"I suppose so."

"Great. Shall we go?"

They stood up shakily. He held the door for Rita as they stepped outside, leaving the warmth of the Catfish behind. It was the middle of December and cold.

"To the stars through difficulty."

"What?"

"Our state motto." She licked her lips, stuck her hands deep in her pockets, tried to make herself warm. "To the stars through difficulty."

"So where we headed?" Rick asked.

"Indiana Street. The sixteenth block of Indiana Street."

She'd moved into the blue house on Ohio with Ned and Hank and Betsy just a few weeks after she first smoked marijuana. Six months later, just before Ned and Hank left for California, she'd moved out of the blue house and into a room on Indiana Street, a block away.

The woman who rented the room next to Rita's, Martha, ate mostly macrobiotic foods, and the kitchen they shared smelled of brown rice frying and tahini. She told Rita that macrobiotics means "great life." She said that eating grains, tofu, tempeh, vegetables, and fruits could free you to live a life of joy and health.

Rita had moved out of the blue house because by that point, she knew nothing was going to happen between her and Hank, much as she might want it to. Sometimes, to make herself feel better, she'd sit in the kitchen she shared with Martha and fry up a big bowl of rice.

Once, she and Hank tried to make love on the waterbed that took up most of the floor in Ned's room there. People came and went at that house, staying as long as they needed a place to stay. That night, when she and Hank were alone, they smoked a joint and lay on Ned's bed. They lay next to each other, on their backs. Their fingers touched. For a long time they lay there without saying anything. Rita wanted Hank, but she didn't say it. She wanted him to lean over her and kiss her and press himself against her. When she was just thinking that nothing was going to happen, Hank moved.

The water in the bed shifted, and Rita felt herself tighten up, mentally try to grab hold of something. All she could think of were the waves she'd once seen off U.S. 1 when she'd gone to Carmel as a child with her parents. She hadn't wanted to run into the waves the way her tall father did. So she stood knee-deep in the surf, afraid that if she went too far she'd be pulled from everything she knew and had counted on in life up to that moment. So she'd turned back to shore.

The waterbed worried Rita, too, the way its waves forced her to give in to them. So she stiffened when the clear mattress swelled and rose, but Hank was up above her then and kissing her on the mouth, harder than the first kiss he'd given her after *Easy Rider*. He lowered himself on top of her. She pressed her pelvis against his and after a while, longer than she'd expected, he pressed back.

Something was wrong.

"Are you all right?" Rita whispered.

He didn't answer.

They lay that way for a time, then he climbed off her and they lay again on their backs next to each other, holding hands. Rita was afraid she was going to cry. She was afraid it was her, the same terrible flaw that had sent her out of the Pacific surf back to the towel where her mother lay on the beach.

In a little while they heard Ned and Betsy come in the front door. Ned made peyote tea and the four of them drank it.

During that long summer evening they roamed the streets of Lawrence: played pinball at the parlor on Massachusetts, listened to music at Lenny Zero's, thought about buying milk at Drake's Bakery and decided against it. They studied the ceramic lawn animals that stood in front of Moon's Variety Store. They went to the laundromat at 7th and Locust where they used plastic tickets instead of coins for the washing machines, and they ended up on top of Pioneer Rock down at the park on 6th.

"Here's a game," Ned Kehde said. "But first I have to tell you about these people I've met. They're involved with a group called More House in California. It's a big family of friends. They buy old warehouses all over the state and fix them up. They make a lot of money and share it. Everybody lives together; everybody shares everything. You get anything you want. All you have to do is ask. You can sleep with anybody you want, you can ask for a TV set, anything. You just make your list.

"So let's pretend we're in More House. What would you ask for? You first, Betsy."

Betsy giggled and tugged at a braid of her hair. "This is hard."

"Come on. Be honest."

"Okay." She undid her braid and ran her fingers through the crimped plaits of hair. "I want… Oh I don't know. You're gonna laugh."

"Do it, Betsy." Ned sounded severe.

"I want a kid. Kids. Pure love."

"'Kay. I buy that. You're next, Hank-o."

Hank jumped down from the rock and ran around it twice, looking up at them all, laughing. He wouldn't stop laughing, and in the dark, his grin looked like a raw wound behind the beard.

"Well?" Ned asked. His pale blue eyes shone like an animal's.

Hank looked at Rita for a minute then looked away toward Ned. His eyes stayed there, resting on Ned's face.

"You," he said.

Hank was still running in place, hands in his pockets. But the grin had disappeared.

Ned was the first to reach out and touch Hank's shoulder, but Rita thought those in-between seconds of stunned silence must have seemed an eternity to Hank. She was embarrassed by how personally hurt she felt, felt herself dropping as though underwater, betrayed.

The rest of the summer, fall and winter, Rita kept hoping Hank's feelings would change. His revelation about Ned hadn't made her stop loving him and seemed, in fact, to sweeten the fight. She grew obsessed, still passionate about someone who didn't want her, who didn't want any girl. Still in love with Hank, Rita wouldn't, couldn't go to bed with anyone else.

Until that night with Rick Thatcher.

When Rita unlocked the door to her room on Indiana Street, Martha stuck her head out to see if she wanted to talk. But when she saw Rick standing there, she said, "G'night," and closed her door.

In Rita's room, a rust and blue India print hung on the wall behind a green sofa bed. A wobbly nightstand held a rose-covered tea cup and saucer from her grandmother and a ceramic ashtray. There was a small table she used as a desk, an old steamer trunk where she kept some of her clothes, and a bentwood rocker. Rita's cat Pookah sat there, sleeping.

As Rick walked in behind her, the room seemed suddenly much too small. She didn't know why she'd decided to move there. Rick walked to the far wall in just three strides, picked up Pookah, dropped her to the floor, and then sat down in the rocker. "Got a beer?" he asked.

"No."

"This'll do," he said and lit a joint he pulled from his shirt pocket. For a few minutes, neither of them spoke; then Rick said, "This guy I know who develops photos at the drug store in Council Grove found a picture of the sheriff fucking his wife. I mean the *sheriff's* wife. Pretty steamy stuff."

"What were they doing?" Rita asked. She was sitting on the floor, cat in her lap.

"I'll show you." And he stood up and took off his flannel shirt and jeans then leaned over to pull Rita up next to him. He unbuttoned her blouse and lifted it over her shoulders. When he unsnapped her jeans she shivered.

He circled her waist with his hands.

"You're shivering," he said.

"I'm cold," she answered.

"I'll warm you," he said. "I'll do whatever you want."

THE JEWEL BOX

This is what Sarah whispered in her grandmother's ear:

"Inside the Jewel Box there were crystal clear pools with bright slipping shadows of fish: mudskippers, seahorses, Missouri-bred salamanders. Above them, steel arches that mirrored the smooth, easy curve of the Gateway Arch. Windows that let in a great deal of light, and left a fine white wash on the walls.

"There were tropical trees, waterfalls, and fountains, and below us, golden pheasants and flamingos flashed among the bushes and streams. In the trees, there were scarlet ibis. A touch pool, with turtles and crayfish."

Nini lay on a small bed, too close to the floor. Sarah wasn't even sure her grandma was listening. It had been forty years since the two of them had taken the trip to the St. Louis Zoo. Sarah had been just a girl. She remembered how fast the train had moved, how quickly rows of corn and fields freckled with brown cows had rushed past the window.

A lean tree outside Nini's room at the nursing home bowed in the wind.

Nini weighed 76 pounds. She wouldn't eat. She was dying. A blue plastic band circled her wrist, naming her. Her white hair was ripe with the smell of shampoo, and dark bruises floated under her eyes. Her gown was covered with small blue birds.

Sarah wanted her grandma to be able to let go, to die peacefully with her there. She wanted to help the transition.

Although when Nini's stomach growled, Sarah's ears ate up the rumblings, glad for this small sign of life.

"Do you remember?" Sarah whispered urgently into the nearly translucent ear.

They'd taken the train from Kansas City Union Station. When the train pulled from the platform, Sarah watched her parents grow smaller and smaller. It was the first time and she was leaving them behind, the first time she'd set out for somewhere unknown.

On board, she sat prim and happy next to Nini. The weekend trip to St. Louis had been a present for Sarah's tenth birthday. They'd visited the Veldt with its swampy alligator pool, the zoo with its Rose Garden and Jewel Box, a huge wrought iron and glass conservatory filled with plants and birds.

Sarah wanted to remind her grandmother of that magical trip, to take them both back to that earlier time and maybe convince her that the place where Nini was now headed might, just might, be as dazzling, as teeming, as safe.

"Birds flew in and out among the branches. Plants grew everywhere, and tall grasses waved in an unseen wind." Sarah paused. "Maybe that's what Heaven is like," she said, thinking, *it's ok, you'll be safe. It's ok to let go now.*

"Is it real?" Nina asked.

Her voice startled Sarah.

"I don't know," Sarah admitted. "I hope so."

"Well, I'll let you know."

"Take me to the bathroom. I need to go to the bathroom." This from the woman who shared Nini's room, Gretta. She'd been asleep when Sarah walked in but now struggled to stand, one bony hand clutching the open back of her thin gown, the other reaching for a metal walker. Her bare back and bottom were dotted with brown moles.

The bathroom was in the corner of the small room. Sarah turned on the light then waited, uncertain how much help Gretta would need. The old woman walked in by herself, and Sarah closed the door behind her.

"Oh, it hurts," Gretta said, loudly through the door. "I just went a while ago and I have to go again."

"Oh, honey!" Gretta moaned.

Sarah helped her back to bed, but Gretta refused to lie down.

"Nini's my grandma," Sarah told her.

"Oh." Gretta stared through gold-rimmed glasses.

"She's 95 years old."

"I'm 91," Gretta said. "Never thought I'd live this long and don't know why I did."

"Gretta, I think you should lie down."

"Oh honey, that's all I do around here," she said, but she put her legs up on the bed and waited for Sarah to cover them.

Nini had closed her eyes again. The sheet rose and fell with her slight breaths.

In a framed photo on the nightstand, Gretta stood broad-hipped and smiling in a blue-checked dress next to a man just her size. Both wore leis of hibiscus. Behind them, the fronds of a palm tree froze mid-sway.

"My husband died in 1982," Gretta said. "He was sitting next to me on a plane. We were going to visit my nephew in Pennsylvania."

Gretta continued, "Never a sick day in his life. Heart failure on the plane. That was a terrible Christmas."

A nurse brought in a brown cafeteria tray with two cartons. "Now, Gretta, you talkin' this nice lady's ear off?" The nurse wore a navy sweater over her white uniform. "You're my good girl. Now, drink this up fast."

To Sarah, she said, "Your grandma's the fussy one. Just won't eat anymore. Maybe for you, she'll get some of this down. We have to try."

Sarah took the carton and straw the nurse handed her. Eyes pooling.

"It's okay, honey. You know when she won't eat, that's just a sign. She knows it's almost time."

Sarah's tears and nose ran.

"It's in God's hands now," the nurse said. She picked up the tray and smiled. "You let me know what you need now, honey. And Gretta, you let her spend time with her grandma. That's who she's come to see, you know."

Gretta grunted and turned her face to the wall.

Sarah wiped her nose and eyes then knelt beside Nini's bed.

"Somewhere we couldn't see," she whispered through the strands of white hair that floated near her mouth, "we heard birds flying in to rest on the branches of trees."

She touched her grandmother's shoulder, bird-like bones. Nini's paper-thin eyelids rose half-way.

"Nini," she said. "I've got a milkshake for you."

Nini's eyes, watery and pale, stared back at her.

"Look, it's vanilla." Sarah lifted the carton and straw, like a woman in a TV commercial. "Not quite as good as Winstead's but..." She tried to stick the straw between Nini's lips. "You have to," she said.

Again she tried to insert the straw, staring at the tiny bump in the dip of her grandmother's upper lip, and the small growth on the side of her neck that looked like a rice krispie. But Nini wouldn't drink.

"When I was little," Gretta said from her bed, "I had some childhood disease. Oh, what's the name of it. I don't remember now. The doctor came every day to my mama's house to rock me in his arms. Rock me. Rock me in his arms."

Sarah squeezed Nini's hands. The old woman's eyes shut again.

"Never thought I'd get this old," Gretta continued. "Who wants to be 91?"

After a while, an aide walked in, wearing bunched-up socks and hiking boots, a green sweatshirt and a gold cross. "There's a birthday party," she said to Sarah. "Maybe your grandma would eat a piece of cake. Maybe since you're here." In one swift motion, she lifted Nini in her arms, the cross swinging between them, and deposited her in her wheelchair. Nini looked like a petulant child woken from a nap.

"Edith, you can't sleep all day on me here!" the aide chided. "Birthday party time! Come on out with your granddaughter and have some cake."

Nini pinched the back of the aide's hand. "No-o," she cooed softly. But there was a twinkle in her eye, the look she used to give Sarah whenever they were ready to escape some boisterous family gathering and go off on an adventure alone.

"I'm Carol," the aide said. "Your grandma's a feisty one. She lets us know just what she likes and what she doesn't. But she's sweet. My is she sweet. Always a smile. She just knows what she likes. Why, sometimes when you put her in the wheelchair, and she doesn't want to go, she just puts her feet down. Stops right like that." Carol motioned for Sarah to push the wheelchair and follow her out the door. "That's why she's holding on so long, I bet. Some of them don't."

"Nini worked in a hospital for twenty-five years, as a surgical technician," Sarah began, but Carol was already far ahead of them, near a long decorated table in the cafeteria.

Half a dozen wheelchairs circled the table, and other nursing home residents had gathered. Some sat upright and dressed, others slumped in their seats in pale pajamas. Carol turned on a boom box. Nini's pink-slippered feet hit the linoleum, and the wheelchair jerked to a stop.

"It's the birthday party," Sarah said. "Remember? We were going to have cake?"

Nini's claw fingers reached up for Sarah's. There'd been so many birthday parties: beautiful doll cakes Nini had decorated with tiered pink-icing-dresses, special gifts like Sarah's first Brownie camera, and the Happy Hospital doll with plastic crutches and stick-on measles.

Sarah squeezed her grandma's hand, then had to pretend to be busy so Nini wouldn't see her cry. "I'll get that chair over there so I can sit right by you."

Nini's head nodded like the head of a dandelion gone to seed.

When Sarah came back, Carol was holding a piece of cake. Nini smiled and patted Carol's hand.

"I love your grandma," Carol said, her tan hand steady beneath Nini's ghostly one. "We have lots of good talks, don't we, Edith?"

Sarah tried to think of something else she could give her grandma. Something else she remembered from their trip: "At the Jewel Box, there'd been Bali mynahs, fruit doves, red lories. Birds flying all around us."

Carol set the plate on Nini's lap. "It's orange cake. For Eleanor's birthday."

"This looks so good. Can I give you a bite?" Sarah asked Nini.
Nini nodded.

Sarah cut into the cake, loading the plastic fork with plenty of icing. The fork came out of Nini's mouth clean. She smiled.

Sarah gave her another bite. And another.

"Would you like another piece?"

"Yah-us," Nini drawled. She ate another few bites then held up her hand and said, "No more."

Sarah moved a Styrofoam cup of coffee back and forth beneath Nini's nose. She sniffed with interest, and her fingers circled the cup.

"Be careful, it's hot."

Nini sipped while Sarah held the cup. "I like it hot," Nini said happily, sitting straight in her chair. "Your mother, my. I never saw anyone drink so much coffee in my life."

Sarah was too shocked at the powers of caffeine to answer. In a minute, she lifted the cup again, but Nini's chin was down. She patted her grandma's soft hair. She used to have her hair done once a week, without fail, walking from her apartment down Brush Creek to a shop on the Plaza.

Sarah looked around the room, suddenly frantic. They knew no one at this birthday party. It was stuffy in the room; the windows were streaked. The paper party cloth looked pathetic now, ripped and stained with spills. One woman in a wheelchair had a bit of icing on her nose; no one had noticed or wiped it clean.

"Let's get out of here." Sarah rubbed Nini's brow. "I can push you in the wheelchair outside. Some fresh air would be good."

Nini's slippers remained on the footrest.

If I can just get her outside, to a different place, Sarah thought. *Let the sun fall on her, bring her back to me. Maybe it's not time for her to go and it's my own arrogance that wants to speed her along.*

The wheelchair rolled noisily down the hall, past fuzzy stick-up decorations: purple and yellow pansies tied with a white bow, a heart pierced by an arrow.

Finally, they reached the front lobby. A big-screen TV blared.

Sarah maneuvered the wheelchair through the glass door that led to the inner vestibule and hesitated; her stomach sank. The sun was simply too bright, the wind too strong. It would be too much for Nini, she knew it. And Nini's chin had fallen forward again as though she were asleep.

So Sarah pulled the wheelchair back into the lobby. Nini's head stayed down as Sarah pushed her back down the terrible, long hall toward the music still playing in the cafeteria. She parked the wheelchair, pulled up a chair, and they sat listening to "Paper Moon" and "Orange Colored Sky" and "Time to Get Ready for Love." On the last song, Nini kept time with one knurly finger, just as she'd done singing Sarah to sleep as a child.

Sarah swayed the wheelchair back and forth, slightly at first, then more pronounced. Rocking her, rocking her.

She slipped her arm beneath Nini, who curled up easily when Sarah lifted her, light as a feather. One scoop, and Nini was out of the rocker; one step, and Sarah was back in her chair with her grandma on her lap.

Carol frowned, stepping forward to stop them.

But Nini was smiling, and they were swaying to the rhythm. Back and forth, back and forth.

"There were black-footed penguins swimming in a pool," Sarah whispered. "Gliding back and forth, back and forth."

Nini's eyes finally closed, but only to sleep.

Two weeks later, in another town, Sarah woke from a dream. Gold spheres of light, bursting like fireworks, had flown through her room, passing over the heads of her sleeping dogs and four-poster bed. All around her, there'd been shadows on the walls. Dark shadows of fish, large ones and small, smooth against the pink and blue flowered paper. The shadows of an eel, curving through water, seahorses and tall grasses, wide-winged birds.

Sarah sat upright, knees to her chest, and began to rock. Rocking and remembering until the sun rose and the phone rang with news of the passing Nini had already shared.

THE YOGI AND THE PEACOCK

Now I'll never admit to being a good Catholic, but my name is Jim McDermott and the boys down at the tub and tile warehouse call me the Big Babboo. I got most things going for me—a woman I'm not living in sin with, a kid (I never had but the one son), and a fine hole of a place above the video club. Still, things get slow: When God made time, he made plenty of it. Most days I wake up, I know what's going to happen. Like I been here before.

But something changed all that. And I'm not sure if it's what I think it was or something else entirely. Mind you, most things stay the same. I wake up in the mornings, I can count on my powdered-sugar doughnuts. I can count on Alma sitting across the kitchen table from me. And I can count on a couple of cups of steaming black coffee. Usually, I'll have the newspaper held straight up in front of me so I don't have to see Alma's fat face. Not that my woman's ugly, her face is her own, but—. By the very nature of things, and so my boys at the warehouse figure, once you've seen someone for twenty-three years there's small chance they'll start looking better.

Not that Alma doesn't try.

Seems like she and her girlfriends spend half their lives gussying up at the beauty parlor down the street. Georgio's it's called, though I know for a fact the guy that runs it is the same guy I knew back in Troop 29, George DeBanca. He was a big galoot then and probably still is now, only now he's got this head of tight blond curls and a long, skinny moustache he coats with wax. Cripes. Still, I know as well as the next man that no man knows the soul of another.

Most of my chums from Troop 29 stayed right here in the old neighborhood like me. Nothing much changed. We got bigger bellies, bigger butts, sadder faces. Sure, things get slow.

But on the morning I want to tell you about, I was going at my doughnuts nice and easy, picking them out of the box and popping them into my mouth, then brushing the sugar powder off my pants leg. I had the paper held right up in front of me but I can tell you for a fact what was going on behind it. Because I could hear Alma's chair leg make that rude noise scraping the linoleum just like it does every morning. Then I could hear Alma's slippers shuffling over to the cabinets, where I could hear her pull something down. I didn't even have to look, I knew what it was even before the lid of the canister fell on the counter. Whatever else may ail it, sometimes you've got to give marriage its due: at least you don't have to look.

Usually I'll listen to Alma shuffle back to the table, pour a spoonful of real sugar into her coffee, and throw the envelope of fake stuff back into the bowl. Maybe she leaves those pink envelopes out there on the table so her friends can see them. Or maybe so she'll get thin just because they're there. Don't that beat all?

But this one morning I'm talking about, I hear the chair yelp as it scrapes the floor, I hear the swish of Alma's slippers, but I don't hear any of the rest of it. In fact, I don't even know if Alma's back sitting across from me because my eye's been caught by this ad:

WITHOUT NEO-CERE, YOU WILL DIE UNFUFILLIED.
WITHOUT EXPERIENCING LIMITLESS JOY,
PROSPERITY, POWER, PSYCHUOUS SEX!

I bring the paper up closer to read:

The Neo-Cere discovery can lead you to a personal renaissance.
Based on centuries-old techniques, so simple and yet so
encompassing, the Neo-Cere techniques are fully revealed in
the Data Packet we will send you for only $3.97. Surprisingly
easy, amazingly powerful, these secrets of the masters will give

you everything you need for mental peace, financial security, psychuous sex, and romantic love. Write for the booklet, Dept. OM, Institute for Neo-Cerebral Studies, Boca Raton, FLA 33432. NO OBLIGATION, NO RISK.

Now don't ask me why this particular ad caught my eye this particular morning. Maybe it was the noise of that chair. Maybe it was knowing Jim Jr. was going to hit me up later that day for seventy-five bucks to fix the bike he smashed up running straight into a brick wall. It wasn't even a big ad, not much to look at, but damn if I didn't stare: PSYCHUOUS SEX. PROSPERITY. PEACE, once and for all.

About three weeks later, I got a little book in the mail that's filled with photographs of Indians, *East* Indians, with their eyes closed and their legs folded like nothing I've ever seen or ever could do.

I flipped through the pages a couple of times. I didn't know much about this sort of thing at the time but I had heard about meditation before. It looked to me like the book was nothing more than a Few Easy Steps to Meditate. Only it wasn't with the prayers Father O'Dwyer had given us when we were kids but with long strings of letters.

Instead it looked like with these mantras you had a choice: If you wanted to get rid of some bad habits, say, you'd chant *Om na-ma-see-vaa-ya.* If you were in trouble, needed some outside help, you'd say *Om-muh-me nah-me nah-rai-uh-no-uh.* And if all you wanted to do was relax, all you had to say was *Om.* Which sounded easy enough to me.

Still, that first day, I remember throwing the book at the wall. I was so mad at getting ripped off.

But then one night that next week, while Alma was sleeping next to me with her hair in those god-awful pink foam rollers, I kept tossing and turning, tossing and turning. I kept thinking about the guys my boy Jim Jr. was hanging out with, with their torn black t-shirts that said Megadeath, their erupted faces and cigarettes and earrings.

My eyes kept going back to where that silly little book still lay on the floor where I'd thrown it. There was a little jar of Alma's

"Midnight Mocha" nail polish that had fallen off the dresser and lay right beside the book. I just kept looking at them both and thinking about Jim Jr. Then, since I knew I wasn't going to sleep that night anyway, I got up, got the book, and took it out to read in the living room where I wouldn't wake Alma.

I read the whole thing straight through.

From outside my window, this BEER sign kept flashing neon-red over all the pages.

When I'd finished, I closed the book and flipped it onto the coffee table and put my feet up beside it. I closed my eyes. I started saying one of those mantras, but then I had to reach over to the book again to see if I was saying it right. I'd picked a short one, but not *Om*. I figured that one was just too easy, how could it do any good? Maybe it's the way I was brought up. "You'll not pray in vain," the priest had said.

So I said the words to myself maybe ten times in a row and then I started thinking about Paulie, Jim Jr.'s friend who's always walking around quoting some band called Jonathan Richman and the Modern Lovers. It was a poor thing for a boy to be relying on at the beginning of his manhood. When I realized I'd started thinking about Paulie, I pulled myself up short and started saying the mantra again, this time out loud: *Aye-ee-mah*.

I don't know, that first night, I was disappointed.

Nothing happened. There was no shattering glass, no blinding light. I'm all for being patient, but a man reaches a point. So I got up, headed into the kitchen, let out a holy oath when I stubbed my toe in the dark, and pulled a Bud out of the icebox.

About a week later, when Alma was out playing pinochle with her girlfriends, I went and sat on the edge of our unmade bed, closed my eyes, and figured I'd give it another try.

Only this time, I sat with my hands folded on my lap like I did at St. Ambrose sitting next to Mom. Don't think I didn't feel a little funny sitting there on that bed like I used to do in church. I remember when I was little, moving around like I had to get up and go to the bathroom *now*. I remember scratching my nose, my ear, anything to be *moving*, doing something. Anything not to have to listen to Father O'Dwyer tell me about the guilt that had been laid on my soul before I even had much of a choice in the matter.

"Do you expect me to die covered with my sins?" I asked Alma when we first married. She'd taken a poor view of all the time I spent at church. So finally I stopped.

So now here I was sitting on this mess of a bed like I was praying only all I was really trying to do was hold on to that blessed mantra. *Aye-ee-ma*. It seems like I can't hold on to it at all. Like it was one of those fish Jimmy and I used to try and catch when he was a boy, the silver ones, *the slippery ones*, too small even to make the whole thing worthwhile, but they had this blue spot between their eyes like a moonstone. I think both Jimmy and I thought if we caught one, everything would be all right from then on out, if we could only hook those beauties.

Then I started thinking about Jimmy, about the vitamin jar I found stuffed in his pocket with grass and a few cocoa-colored pills laid out on top. Bloody fool. I don't mind if he uses the stuff, the grass that is, but when he goes and busts up his bike, when he cusses out his Mom in a blue streak and don't say nothing at all to me, then I've got to worry. So I start thinking about Jimmy and before Jimmy and about how my young Alma McDermott had looked so beautiful out on Coney Island when Jimmy was just a boy. My arms would be wrapped around my wife's white shoulders, they were so thin like a bird, I could feel the bones.

Aye-ee-ma. Aye-ee-ma.

In a while, I remembered what the book had said about trying to picture a candle flame lit in the dark.

I could see the candles, a whole row of them in fact, lined up at the back of an altar. I could hear the whispering of pages as they turned and I could see the light from the candles shimmering over brass plates and pretty soon I felt my head fall forward and my mouth drop open, just the way it used to against Mom's lap.

Then the months went by. Eight, maybe more. I kept on meditating and I tell you my mind was easier for it. I'd handed myself over to it, body and bones. Maybe because it was something to do when things got slow. It wasn't anything to tell Alma or my chums down at the warehouse about, even though they've known me since I was a kid. But later at night when I couldn't sleep, when I'd be staring up at the cracks in the ceiling thinking that the lifeblood of this place was seeping out of those cracks just as plain as if somebody opened up a vein, then I'd do it. Or in the dead of the afternoon when Alma was down the street getting her hair teased and tangled, when I was off shift and the street was quiet, then I'd go sit in the living room and meditate.

Some days it worked, some days it didn't.

But things did start happening.

I don't know.

I kept having these experiences.

For instance, late in October I decided to take Jim Jr. to the movies on Saturday afternoon. Just us boys, I tell him. I picked the movie. I picked *The Right Stuff* because it would have been nice for Jim Jr. to still do something with his life. Maybe he can pick up a little hero worship, I thought; maybe he can't find it in his old man. So we went into the movie with a tub of popcorn and a box of chocolate-covered raisins.

While we were watching, every once in a while I'd take advantage of the dark to sneak a look over at my boy. Then once, when I looked back at the screen, I saw something funny. One minute I was watching a test pilot with movie-star looks sitting in the cockpit of a needle-nose plane then next thing I know I'm looking at a crowd of folks who look like they don't have any business being anywhere near an Air Force base.

I blink, but when I look again I see myself right up there on the screen with them and all of us are standing in this large, dark room.

Now, none of these people look like they're from my neighborhood. And they don't look like they have anything to do with Chuck Yeager or the movie star that's playing him. I *know* what they look like. One guy's in a long robe and has this black cap pulled over his ears. He's lifting his finger and pointing at me, showing me where to stand. Behind him, a huge crucifix runs from floor to ceiling.

There's some scuffling, then somebody grabs my arm and I watch on the screen as this whole crazy crowd of people pushes me outside into a yard. Where there's some scaffolding. And a guillotine. And I sit right next to my son in this god damn movie theater and watch on the screen as somebody leads me up the steps, bends me over and . . .

It knocked me right into the middle of next week.

And I don't think Jimmy saw it.

When the other movie came back on I couldn't move in my seat. The credits rolled by. And then I stood up and walked up the aisle with Jim Jr. He said he wanted to stop at the john and while I waited in the lobby, I notice I've still got my hand up at my collar.

That night, I lay in bed thinking about a lot of things.

About how much I've always hated shaving in the morning. How I always like putting that cool foamy cream on my face, thinking each time it will be okay, that if I just feel that cool wet cream on my face then quick bring the razor up all will be well. But every time, it never was any different, I'd panic when I finally brought the razor to my throat. I'd stand there staring in the steamed-up mirror and my eyes would look like a trapped animal's. Or a sinner's behind the confessional grille.

Then I started to think about how I never had liked knives. How I always made Alma carve the Easter ham or the Christmas turkey, always made some excuse.

And now here I see this Vision. And I've got to think even Father O'Dwyer himself would have to call it that.

And I don't know what to make of it.

About a week or two later, I was walking home from the warehouse with some of the boys. We saw this skinny girl with tight jeans and a bluebird tattooed on her arm. She was just coming out of a store that had a sign up above the door that said YES! Books.

After I left the guys, I walked back to the store. I asked the first person I saw, a boy behind the counter with a tiny scar above his lip, if he might know anything about meditation. He pointed me toward an aisle in the back. I walked back and started looking at all the books until I saw one that said *REINCARNATION: Cutting the Veil of Ignorance.*

I read some of it just standing there. I knew I couldn't take it home with me, there'd be the devil to pay. When I saw the guy at the front of the store looking back at me, I put the book away and walked out fast, like I had other business.

After that, the meditations kind of quieted down, but sometime in November I saw that the Neo-Cere book was gone from where I'd hidden it behind the pipes under the bathroom sink. Right around December, Alma started sitting with me in the living room in the evenings, on the TV chair across from my couch, meditating. Neither of us ever said a word about it.

Until one afternoon, when Alma was sitting there across from me. I started getting this funny feeling, really hot, like I was burning up. I could feel sweat start rolling down my forehead and I could see the soles of my feet swell and start to bleed. I smelled burning flesh and if I didn't know better I'd think it was me who was being roasted alive.

I could see Alma's eyes open and go wide.

And later that night, when we were finally lying in bed, she told me she'd seen it, too.

She said it had looked like me but wasn't me. She said she'd seen flames all around me and a stack of brushwood and charcoal beneath me. She said she saw a cross in the background, covered with black crepe.

I didn't say a word.

But cripes. Mother of God.

Since then, no matter what I'm doing, I keep hearing Father O'Dwyer's voice in my head going on about Hell and Damnation. It's like he's talking just to me. I keep hearing the sound the beads made, their neat, quiet clicks, as my mother counted her rosary over and over again rocking on the porch swing before we'd walk to evening mass.

And I feel spooked. Just last week, I come home and Alma says she's got a surprise for me. "Look out the window," she says, pointing down at the street. I look over and there in the vacant lot across the street, there's this *peacock*.

"I bought it," Alma says to me. "I bought the peacock and then I bought baling wire and posts and made a pen. I asked Ed, the guy who manages the video club downstairs, if I could keep it across the way. Ed says, 'Fine, keep it there, maybe it'll bring in more business.'"

Alma tells me she bought the peacock so she could have more color in her life.

Then Jim Jr. walks into the kitchen where we're standing and tells me Michael Jackson says that of all the bird families, the peacock's the only one to integrate all the colors into one.

Now don't get me wrong.

I've got nothing against a little color in our lives.

I've got nothing against rearranging the status quo, shining in a little bright light where everything was dark before.

But still, I've decided I'm going to have to give this place, this Neo-Cerebral Institute, a call.

Because I just don't know what it is I got myself into. I just don't know what it is I've seen.

Today I finally manage to get a phone number for them from the long-distance operator in Boulder, for this Department OM. And I give them a call.

"Look," I say, "today when I go into the living room my wife, Alma's her name, is sitting on the back of our couch. She's got her hair down and she's completely naked. She's got her hair dyed blond and it's hanging over her shoulders and she's sitting on the back of our couch side-saddle.

"I'm here on the phone talking to you," I say to them, "and I think I want this all to stop."

While I'm on the phone, I look over at my wife and our eyes meet. Our eyes meet.

"Can you tell me what this is supposed to mean?" I ask the person at the other end of the line. "Do you know where this is all going to go? Is there anybody there who can help us?

"I've got this wife, see, I've got this peacock, and I've got these sleepless nights."

The person on the other end hangs up.

I walk over to where Alma's sitting on the couch. She reaches out and takes my hand, gives it a squeeze. She smiles at me; I smile back. We'll just have to see where it goes from here.

THE SECOND TIME
THE BIRD ESCAPED

The neighbor's peacock let out a long, high-pitched cry from behind its large wired pen. The neighbor, who might or might not know about the separation, waved to Caroline through the evening's steadily falling snow. She waved back then knocked on the door of her soon-to-be former home. An unfamiliar silver Mazda hunched in the circle driveway.

Caroline didn't know if she wanted to cry, pee, or both. She'd just left an Indian restaurant where, while dining with her brother, she'd downed far too many Kingfisher beers.

Her brother's MS had taken a turn for the worse. His speech slurred, and he'd had trouble swallowing. Twice, he dropped his fork.

Caroline needed to know more about the debilitating disease, and she needed to ask Trey. Now. The combination of her brother's physical and her own emotional unraveling was really too much to bear. Trey's specialty was infectious disease but still, he would know far more about her brother's prognosis than anyone else she knew.

She lifted the brass knocker—a circle formed by two hands holding a fat heart—and let it fall again. She'd polished that knocker to a high sheen when she'd first moved into Trey's house, which stood on a quiet country road outside of Tarrytown.

The door opened. Trey's normally ruddy face lost its color. Caroline knew she looked like shit. She'd dressed for dinner but that one last check in the rearview mirror revealed streaked mascara. Trey, on the other hand, looked great. He wore the long-sleeved black polo she'd given him last Christmas. He always looked good in it.

She started to compliment him but noticed movement over his shoulder: someone rising from one of two club chairs that sat in front of the television in a way Caroline had never positioned them. It was Amber, Trey's new girlfriend.

We never sat and watched TV like that, Caroline thought.

From where she still stood on the front stoop, she could see a fire burning in the fireplace. She pulled her down jacket close, shivering. "I need to talk to you," she whispered, hoping the sound of the TV would keep Amber from hearing.

"Amber's here," he said.

"I know." Then, more loudly, "I don't care. I need to talk to you. Something's happened."

Amber had reached them. She stood with her hands on the hips of her black cigarette jeans, her fingers flared toward the front. The volume on the TV suddenly ratcheted up: "More snow predicted. Travel warning issued throughout tri-state area."

Amber looked back at the TV, her chin-length blond hair swinging as she turned. "Driving's going to be bad very soon."

"So?" Caroline asked Trey. "Can I come in?"

Trey blinked. "Oh Jesus sorry." He moved away from the door and Caroline stepped inside.

"Hi," she said. "I'm sorry. I just…"

Trey took another step back to stand halfway between Caroline and Amber then cleared his throat.

"I'm sorry," Caroline couldn't remember if she'd said this before. Her words sounded almost slurred even to her ears. "I didn't mean to interrupt."

"You OK?"

Ever since she'd moved out of the house—after Trey refused both to budge and to stop his affair and his rages—she'd learned how easy it was to lie, especially when someone asked her how she felt. "Depressed" just wasn't a word people wanted to hear.

Before leaving, she'd tried for a long time to live with his affair and the rages. Sometimes he'd tell Caroline that she was the one he really loved. But somehow it just didn't ring true, and she didn't like him implying that it was her fault he had to cheat.

Now Amber stuck out a mauve-manicured hand and Caroline moved forward to shake it. They each nodded—like a toreador approaches a bull, Caroline thought, though she wasn't sure which of them held which role.

The weather alert on the TV had stopped and the movie Amber and Trey must have been watching had started again: something with Owen Wilson.

Amber fingered the v of her white cableknit sweater. "Trey, why don't you offer Caroline a glass of wine?"

Trey raised his brows. "Do you want wine?"

Caroline knew she shouldn't. "Sure."

They moved to the sitting room. Twenty-four years ago, when she, Caroline, had just become mistress of the house, Trey's first wife, Jenny, had been sitting on the couch where Amber now sat; Jenny had moved out of her marriage house when she and Trey divorced but had come back to pick up her kiln.

Caroline could still remember how nervous she'd been, worried what Jenny would think of the changes she'd made to the house.

Caroline lifted the Baccarat glass Trey gave her, a wedding gift from Trey's mother. "Cheers," she said.

"So," he said, finally sliding back more comfortably into the couch. "What's up?"

"I just came from dinner with Bobby," she said, trying to block Amber out of her line of vision. "He's so much worse. His hands shake. He dropped his fork twice. He looked awful but you know him; not a complaint out of him but I am worried. Very worried. What will he do? What can he do?"

Trey set his glass on the side table then looked back up at Caroline.

"I'm sorry to hear that. It's come on rather quickly, hasn't it?" He frowned down at his lap as though deciding on his next words. "It's worse in men, especially at his age. Medication may help. The progression of the disease may slow down. You just never know."

He looked at Caroline's face, which she knew looked stricken.

"Look, there can be relapses where his symptoms fade and do not come back for years."

She sniffled. She should have brought tissues. "Are you sure?"

"Positive. You—he just has to take it day by day. Some people live with it for years without adjusting their lifestyle too much. If and when he needs to, he can get a cane."

"The doctor already told him to get one."

Trey sighed. "OK. Then he'll get one and learn to use it. Lots of people do. He'll manage."

But Caroline really didn't believe him. She heard Owen Wilson's drawl from the other room. He'd just tried to commit suicide last week. She couldn't remember how.

Caroline closed her eyes and felt dizzy again. No more wine, she told herself, and set her glass down on the floor beside her chair.

Trey was still looking at her. She wished she looked better but his eyes were kind, not hateful like they'd been so many times the last year.

Then he pulled his eyes away. "I'll give him a call. Do you know who his doctor is now?"

"Someone in the city." The name escaped her.

"Find out. And I'll get some recommendations, too." He glanced at Amber then Caroline and cleared his throat loudly. "So, where did the two of you eat?"

Trey loved to eat at great restaurants. Caroline had enjoyed doing that with him and wondered how many of their favorites he'd already shared with Amber. Her chest hurt.

She said, "Malabar."

"Can't stomach it there very often there," Trey said.

"I love Indian food," Amber said. "There's a great place in Soho called Bengal Tiger. Great tikka masala."

Caroline knew she'd never go there.

"Bad tuberculosis outbreak in Mumbai right now," Trey said. "Twelve people. Neither first- nor second-choice drugs worked. Essentially incurable with the medicines we have now." He headed toward the wine cabinet to get another bottle. "Of course the substandard care over there makes it worse. Makes it easy for the superbugs."

Caroline had always wanted to go to India but Trey usually preferred to stay in less exotic places—France, Italy, the Caribbean. Perhaps he was right, she thought. Perhaps his knowledge of all the dangers out there—infections, disease—made his wariness understandable.

"What are you working on now?" she asked.

"Writing a paper on ethical challenges in drug-resistant diseases. And I've got a conference in San Francisco next month."

Amber would probably go with him, Caroline realized. She picked up her glass; she took another gulp, the wine tipping dangerously.

Out the window she saw the neighbor's peacock strutting slowly through their backyard.

"Oh no...it got loose again!" She stood to walk to the tall window as though she still lived there. Trey and Amber joined her.

This was the second time the bird had escaped the neighbor's large penned yard.

It was running now, maybe 10 or 15 miles an hour.

"Last time he spent the night up in that tree, remember?"

She realized he was trying to reminisce with her, the way he had reminisced that long-ago night with Jenny about their honeymoon drive to California in a Day-Glo van.

The peacock stopped, its long tail down, its neck an iridescent blue-green.

"A peacock escaped the Central Park Zoo last summer," Amber said.

Caroline didn't like to think of peacocks in zoos. She'd seen them roam freely at an ashram she'd visited before she met Trey. There'd been peacocks everywhere. She'd learned that the colors of their feathers depended on the angle at which they were seen, that they changed and shimmered depending on how you looked at them.

Amber interrupted her thoughts. "It was on the loose on the Upper East Side and perched on a fifth-floor windowsill. Finally it flew back to its mate at the zoo."

"I'm sure this guy will, too," Trey said.

"Why on earth would he go back to be caged up like that again?" Caroline asked.

As Trey turned, his shoulder touched hers. And once again, she wanted his arms around her. If only things hadn't gotten so bad.

As if sensing what Caroline was thinking, Amber spoke. "They're very territorial, you know. Especially when you put two females together."

"Right," Caroline said and put her glass down on the credenza she'd bought last year.

"So what are you going to do about the bird?" Amber asked Trey.

"It'll go back home; that's what it did last time. It'll want its food and it knows where to go to get it."

The mention of food reminded Caroline of her brother and why she had been stupid enough to put herself in this terrible situation.

"I've got to go," she said. "I want to call Bobby and have to go home."

Trey looked startled again.

Amber put her arm behind Caroline, not touching her but still somehow pushing her toward the door. "I hope your brother will be ok," she said.

Caroline shook her head to clear the cobwebs, the Kingfishers, then started moving toward the door, Amber at her back, Trey lagging behind.

That night 24 years ago when Trey's first wife had visited, Caroline had felt like a third wheel. Because the two people sitting on the couch across from her had so much history behind them. When the evening had ended, Caroline held back while Trey walked Jenny to the door and into the dark night.

This time, the dynamics had changed. Amber had taken charge. And this time, Caroline was the interloper. Karma must have caught up with her.

Amber opened the door. Caroline waited there a moment, looking back at Trey, who simply stood with his hands in his pockets. Then she stepped outside into the cold night. The snow was tumbling down much faster now, settling soundlessly on growing drifts. How on earth would her brother manage his cane in the snow? How on earth could she get home safely?

She turned to see if Trey was still there, but the door to the house had already closed.

NEWS FEED

While her son was in surgery Evelyn sat in the waiting room, alone. Her ex was in Tucson with his girlfriend. She'd brought her new phone, a Samsung Galaxy S3, in from the car with her, played with it ever since Jason had left with the nurse.

It's only supposed to take 45 minutes. But it's already been an hour! I'm worried, she wrote.

A comment appeared almost immediately, from Ruth in Rhode Island. She hadn't seen Ruth in twenty years but they'd caught up recently thanks to Facebook.

Don't worry! He'll be fine.

Another comment, this one from a graphic designer she'd worked with, Monica.

What happened? Before you answer me, go ask the receptionist what's going on. When Bailey had his surgery I bugged the hell out of anybody I could find to get updates.

Evelyn replied quickly.

@Monica, my son cut his hand washing a glass in the sink. Cut a nerve.

OMG. Give him my love. To you too. From @Monica.

Evelyn dropped the phone in her pocket just as the phone in the receptionist's office rang.

The TV in the waiting room was too loud and tuned into an inane morning talk show. Evelyn looked again at the receptionist who sat behind a closed glass window talking soundlessly into her headset.

She lifted her cell from her pocket again to log back on to see if anyone else had commented yet. They had:

Sending wishes for a full and speedy recovery. From Diana, a high school classmate back in the Midwest.

She rubbed her forefinger and thumb together, hard. A new habit she'd acquired since the divorce a year ago. A commercial for anti-depressants came on the TV. Primary colors, flowers blooming, an anthropomorphized sun.

Behind the glass window, the receptionist had removed her headphones. Evelyn stood; one pane of the glass window was pulled back. "Is there a problem with the surgery?" Evelyn asked, hands in her pockets.

"No, not at all. I'm sure the delay means the doctor had to start the procedure late. But if you'd like, I can call down and ask."

Evelyn nodded and returned to her seat as the receptionist closed the glass panel and slid the headset on again. In a moment, the panel separating them slid open again. "No problem at all. I know it's hard to wait when you're the Mom." Jason was 27 so the role of Mom was different now. She pulled out her cell again. A second comment:

Good heavens! I will keep you both in my prayers! Philip, a talented musician she'd met through a mutual friend.

Jason's father should be here, she thought. We should be doing this together. But they weren't.

In all 36 people sent digital wishes, prayers, reiki while she waited. Twenty-three were friends Evelyn had spent time with in the flesh— former neighbors, work colleagues, long-distance relatives. Eight were friends she'd made through Facebook but never met in person. Five messages were from strangers, including one in Belgium.

Every post made her feel better. Facebook now made up an uncomfortably large portion of her social life. If you could even call it that. Just last week, she'd spent New Year's Eve, her first alone since the divorce, with people from California, Maine, Texas, Spain, Italy, Lithuania, and other places around the globe. Even worse, on the stroke of midnight, she'd used her cell phone from bed to exchange wishes with a Twitter connection.

The door to the waiting room opened and a doctor, shorter than Evelyn, walked in wearing royal blue scrubs and cap. A paler blue surgical mask hung from his ears. Evelyn stood again, still clutching the phone in her hand.

"Everything went well," the doctor said, smiling. "I was able to reconnect the nerve. He was lucky the damage wasn't worse."

"I can't believe you can do this so quickly," she said, forgetting her earlier impatience. "I mean, repair a whole nerve."

"Medical technology," he answered. "And teamwork. I'm not the only one in the operating room, remember."

She took a deep breath. "So what do we do now? Will he get feeling back in his hand? Can he eat this afternoon? How long before he goes back to work?" These were the questions Jason's father would have asked, and she knew she had to listen carefully for the answers. She had depended on her husband for so many things, all the practical maneuvers through life.

"We'll give you a sheet of post-op instructions," the doctor said. "And Madeline can take you down to the recovery room now." The receptionist, also smiling, led Evelyn to the stairway. One floor below, Jason sat in what looked like a dentist's chair, an IV in his arm, below his tattoo of the Japanese character for luck. He was happy, relaxed in a way she hadn't seen him for months.

Both the nurse who removed the IV and the beautiful Indian anesthesiologist said Jason had had them all in stitches. "I told him the anesthesia would be like a shot of tequila," the anesthesiologist said. "And Jason said, 'Bring it on!'"

Evelyn spent that night at Jason's apartment. She made mac and cheese, a favorite of his since childhood, adding a few drops of truffle oil—she'd splurged. She washed the dishes in the sink and left them to dry in the red plastic rack. She emptied outdated food from his refrigerator: a carton of orange juice, sour milk, rotten cherry tomatoes, brown-edged lettuce. She'd already filled two large green trash bags but opened one and threw these in on top. Then she stripped his bed, put on clean sheets, made a pile of laundry she could do back at her own house.

Jason sat on the couch with his arm in a cast, elevated. He'd taken two Oxycodone before leaving the surgical center and was still pleasant and unusually talkative. He loved the mac and cheese and couldn't stop saying how much he appreciated her help. This warmed her heart in a way it hadn't been warmed for a long time. Usually Jason was Mr. Independent. He had struggled those first months after the divorce, upping his use of marijuana.

Evelyn convinced him not to use the smoke-stained glass bong on his coffee table. "Not with the pain pills," she said and was happy he listened. She sat on the other couch and they watched three back-to-back episodes of *Law & Order: Criminal Intent*.

Then two of his friends came over. The bong was filled and lit. They offered it to Evelyn, but she said no. The four of them talked about gluten-free diets, the recent shooting, Christian Bale. Evelyn was grateful to be included in their conversation.

The next morning, she took the pile of laundry back to her house, assuring Jason she'd be back soon with clean clothes, beef stew, and a cheesecake. After putting one load in the washer, she sat on the couch in the living room. All she could hear was the hum of the washing machine and the wind chime dinging plaintively from the patio, where snow frosted the furniture and the branches of tall poplar trees. No other houses in sight.

She shifted, so she couldn't see all that empty expanse of land, but that meant she had to face the picture frame on the wall that held photos of her son as a child: Jason in a Barney Halloween costume. Jason crouching under a rocky ledge during the camping trip to New Hampshire. Jason riding a Shetland pony while she, rosy-cheeked and smiling, kept him in the saddle.

Evelyn again rubbed her thumb and forefinger together, reassuring herself that she was still there. Some days this habit was the only physical contact she had.

Cooking for Jason helped pass the time. She realized how long it had been since she'd had someone to cook for and found herself singing as she mixed cream cheese, sour cream, and an egg to pour into a graham cracker crust. The simmering stew filled the kitchen with the delicious smell of broth, sherry, onions.

When the washing machine chimed to say the load was ready, Evelyn threw those clothes in the dryer and the sheets into the washer. Another two hours and she could drive back to Jason's, bearing Mom-type offerings.

Still singing quietly under her breath, she went to the laptop she kept on the kitchen desk. Emails to answer; then, wanting to update her friends about Jason's surgery, she logged into Facebook. She felt proud she hadn't logged in for a while, almost superior. She actually had a life, other things to do besides recording what she was doing! But still, she had to catch everyone up.

> *Jason's doing well. Still some pain and has to hold his arm elevated mostly. Will wear cast for 3 weeks. I had such a good time being at his apartment and will go back this evening probably. Cooking beef stew and cheesecake today, probably a brisket tomorrow. Want to stock him up with prepared meals. I can't tell you wonderful it feels to cook for my grown son again!!!*

She sent a get well post to a friend who'd announced she had the flu and Liked a few other posts: a photo of a puppy with a pink belly, a quote from Rumi, a recipe for gluten-free walnut muffins.

Then she moved to the general News Feed. When she first joined Facebook, she'd tried, successfully, to get a lot of friends, hoping she could use the medium not just to chat but also to promote her work as an illustrator. It hadn't done much good. She'd been out of the mainstream for a while, following where her ex's career led them. She'd done her best to keep up and now was eager to jump back in wholeheartedly. But not a single commission had come from all those connections.

She was now up to 2,651. So when the News Feed scrolled, she saw messages from many people she didn't know. She'd tried to remedy this by moving those she wanted to hear from into a Close Friends list and turning off notices from those she didn't. But this was very time-consuming and most likely one of those jobs that would never be finished.

Scrolling down the feed that afternoon, she stumbled on a post from a man in India named Das Sen-Gupta. She didn't know Das well at all, even by the somewhat low standards for intimacy set by Facebook.

But she could tell from the few posts of his she'd seen that a) he had a good heart, b) he was struggling personally and financially, and c) he made a real effort to post uplifting thoughts for others. He signed many of his posts Miles of Smiles.

Coincidentally, she'd noticed a post from Das a week earlier, before Jason's surgery, saying that it was "time for him to leave this virtual world." At the time she'd been happy for him, imagining he'd met someone and would now be happily engaged in real life. Perhaps a new job or a girlfriend or both.

But the latest post was worrisome. Das's smiling photo was gone, leaving the blank Facebook icon. And someone claiming to be his cousin had written this:

> *Please bad and non-trust people do not respond to this. Request not make fun of this otherwise do not comment on it. Das Sen-Gupta is missing. If anyone of you have his contact number please try to contact him. Last 2 days he is not found. If anyone of you find any information please message me here or send him an email. Thank You to all of his friends.*

Evelyn immediately thought of news stories she'd read about people, mostly teenagers, posting final messages before they committed suicide.

There were already 12 comments to this mysterious post, including responses from its original writer. And even as she watched more kept coming. Some were angry, questioning.

How do we know you're related to Das? This from Audrey Brown in Wichita.

Why do you sometimes say you are his cousin and sometimes his brother?
Stuart Carter in Boulder.

Is this a scam? Wael Newcomb, Liverpool.

Others tried to placate the skeptics. One woman, Betty Eakins, said she'd received a troubling email from Das about how difficult life was for him now. A man, Alex Coaxum, posted a link to a Yahoo news article about a man named Das Sen-Gupta, a vice president at a trading firm, who'd been missing for a week.

Then why had the cousin said he'd only been gone two days? Audrey Brown wondered.

But something was off. Das was hurting for money. Evelyn knew there was no way he was a VP of a trading firm. So she posted that, as well as her prayers and wishes for his return if he truly was gone, trying to stay neutral, unsure herself whether or not to believe whoever was claiming to be Das's cousin or brother. Her comment got two likes.

Responses from the cousin/brother grew more and more impatient and annoyed.

This Das's cousin Shyam. Now all tell me I am hacker!! Not so!! Brother right, no respect I see here. That is why he must of left and isn't found. My English not good but if I true hacker I do bad things, not talk respect. My brother I thought anyone u know where he is… otherwise who not care to come here! No angry!

The posts kept adding up. At one point there were 69. Evelyn sat there, reading each one, hoping Das was okay. As limited, and as digital, as their friendship had been, Das's well-being mattered to her.

All the loneliness of the last year flooded over her. She closed her eyes and pictured all of them—her children young and then young adults, her ex when he loved her and then when he did not, the Facebook friends, whoever they were.

The buzzer on the dryer went off. Evelyn's cell rang. It was Jason, wanting to know when she was coming back to his place with food and clean laundry.

She had thought that if she were sad enough, isolated enough, Jason's father would come back to her, the family would be made whole again. But he had not returned.

He had not returned. And he wasn't going to.

She closed her eyes and, when she heard the wind chime, opened them and stood up. She would go back to Jason's apartment, heat up the stew she'd just made. Put the folded laundry in his dresser. Take those big green bags of old trash out to the curb, ready to be taken away. She knew the bags were both heavy, but somehow she would carry them down the stairs, struggling to balance.

MY LOVERS #1-5, OR WHY I HATE KENNY ROGERS

What follows is by way of explaining what happened last Sunday, when I had more of a brush with sex than I've had in the five years since my divorce. What follows may explain my disappointment.

You see, the first man I fell in love with turned out to be gay and hung himself from a tree along Highway 1 in California.

The second left me when I got pregnant. He was much shorter than me but had lovely lips and gentle eyes.

The third seemed promising: great sex, red-gold hair, tall. We met in a magical way. At a certain time on a certain day of the week, we passed each other going opposite directions on the campus of the University of Kansas. This was the sidewalk near the Student Union, which was burned down by hippies in 1972. I may have known one of the people who did it but I'm not positive about that. If it was the person I'm thinking of, he's now an executive at an insurance company in Florida, with two kids.

Back to how I met #3. When I noticed him walking on campus, near the Student Union, I thought, *That guy's really cute.* He usually wore a jean jacket. Gold wire-rimmed eyeglasses, a red gold beard. He may have worn cowboy boots but I'm not sure.

I do remember that #1, the first man I really fell in love with, who turned out to be gay and killed himself, wore wonderful white tennis shoes. He bounced in them as he walked, and his smile spread all the way across his face.

I know it is unfair to reduce these men, all of whom are as wonderful as people can be, meaning they are imperfect, to numbers. The men I'm telling you about are not men I hate, and in fact I probably don't really hate any men. But sometimes there's a particular gut reaction I have that can feel like hate, or a neighbor of it, like it did last Sunday.

Back to #3. The second time I saw #3, I thought again, *That guy's really cute.* And probably something like, *I'd love to have him as a boyfriend.* Maybe it was something saner, like, *I'd like to get to know that guy and see if we get along.*

The third time we passed each other, #3 smiled at me. He also had a great smile, and his blue eyes crinkled behind those wire rim glasses. He was so tall and lovely!

I smiled back.

We passed each other maybe two more times, smiling wider each time. I started looking forward to seeing him. Then one day he said *Hi* and something else that I know brought joy to my heart but which I can't remember all these years later.

He asked if I wanted to walk to the campanile on campus. I'd lain on the hillside there just the week before, with friends, looking at the sun through a colorful quilt. We'd taken Orange Sunshine on blotters. Everything we saw was in a rainbow; even the colors smelled.

At the campanile, #3 and I talked a lot. Before we parted, he kissed me. He was a great kisser. We dated. We were in love, I'm sure of it. That summer he took a job in La Jolla but we spent long hours on the phone and missed each other's bodies.

That fall, he was back in Lawrence and he was still my boyfriend.

The next thing I remember is me standing at the black phone on the wall at Ginger Sterrett's house. It was late afternoon, December 31. Ginger lived with her pony-tailed boyfriend Ryder who loved jazz and basketball and was smart but not ambitious. I don't think any of us were back then. Many years later, Ginger went home to Bird City, Kansas, and married a rodeo cowboy then divorced.

That December 31, Ginger had handed me the phone. It was #3

calling. I'd assumed he was calling to tell me he was coming over to celebrate New Year's with us. Instead, he said he had met someone and was going out with her that night. I know, I know—I must have been totally blind not to have seen than coming. Later, I would be blind when it came to #4 and #5 as well and then again with what happened last Sunday night.

#3 ended up marrying the girl he went out with that New Year's Eve, which I sometimes told myself made it better. It somehow absolved me of unworthiness.

Many years later, I emailed #3 out of the blue. He'd become a lawyer in D.C. He wrote back right away, saying he still remembered my wonderful smile. That brought me joy.

The relationship with #4 was intense but immoral. Actually those two things go together. Right after I met him, I had the following dream:

I am in a large, sloping green field in a place that looks like England. I walk towards a stone castle up the hill. When I enter the courtyard, a jester with bells on his silk hat hands me an ice cream sandwich. He says, Eat this and you will meet the true love of your life.

I walk back down the hill and sit at a long picnic table. The people sitting with me are people I had just started working with—in real life. The man who had hired me—and became #4—walks up behind me and lays his hand on my shoulder.

For this reason, and others, I fell in love with a married man. I was very ashamed of what we were doing and never once urged him to leave his wife. I thought, *I don't have that right.* But I did seem to assume I had the right to succumb to the most powerful chemistry I'd ever experienced in my life. Many years later, I realized this chemistry was heightened by the illicitness of our affair but still, it was a very intense love, or at least passion, for both of us.

It lasted nine months. #4 now has three children, has been married 35 years, and spends more than half his days working on the other side of the country from his wife. Sometimes I think he should have left her. They didn't have kids at the time we had an affair. In fact, what led to our break-up was his wife getting pregnant. Right, I know I was blind. When I've seen photos of their first-born son he looks sad, and I think that if these things make a difference, this son somehow, on some level, knew that half of the coupling that made him was ambivalent. His younger siblings, both girls, look beautiful, happy, and confident.

Sometimes I wonder if #4 would feel a need to work so far from home if he had married me. I don't know the answer to this, and I often wish I hadn't done what I did.

I had a terrible time with each of the break-ups with #1-#4. I spent months, even years, full of heartache. After each one, I thought, *That's it. There will never be another love.*

I also, at some point during the break-up, got very angry at #2-#4. Not at #1, the one who turned out to be gay and hung himself from a tree along the coast in California.

The summer I was in love with #1, I lived with five people, including him, in a trailer in Steamboat Springs. Sometimes #1 and I lay on a very narrow mattress that basically filled the tiny paneled room that was mine. We would kiss, but nothing more. I assumed this was my fault.

One afternoon the five of us sat at the table in the trailer. We drank peyote tea. It was dark outside when #1 stood up and said, *I'm a homosexual.* We were Midwesterners, and this was 1972.

I immediately ran outside toward the stream that ran through the trailer park. I was crying, loudly. Right, I know that was narcissistic, which is one of several personality disorders I sometimes think I have.

I thought, *How could he do this to me? I am heartbroken. My life is over.*

It wasn't.

#1's life ended 6 months later. Back at school, we had remained friends but I always kept hoping my sexual charisma—weak to begin with—would somehow turn him around and bring his love to me.

Then #1 went to California, for a short stay at a commune with the friend who may have been involved in blowing up part of the Student

Union. That friend wasn't gay. #1's eyes were kind of wild by then, and his smile had grown frantic and too wide.

A week after he flew across the country, another friend came to my apartment in Lawrence—I didn't have a phone, both because of money and principle—and told me #1 had driven north on Highway 1 and hung himself from a tree by the side of the road.

There was terrible, gut-wrenching heartache.

I've read that maybe 9% of Americans have some kind of personality disorder. As I've read some of their descriptions—avoidant, ambivalent, borderline, dependent—I could pretty much see these traits to some degree or another at some time in everybody. And certainly in me.

An interesting fact: in 2005, two psychologists from the University of Surrey compared personality profiles of high-level British executives with those of criminal psychiatric patients. Three personality disorders—narcissistic, histrionic, and obsessive-compulsive—were more common in the executives than the criminals.

#5 is the man who actually turned out to be my true love, in a real way, not fantasy.

He married me, loved me, made me very happy at many times. For nearly 27 years I knew he would never leave me. I loved this. There were other things he did that I didn't love and were, in fact, unacceptable. I don't need to go into those here. Suffice it to say that I ended up being the one to move out though I quickly regretted it and tried hard, begged really, to stay married. Borderline personalities are prone to think, *I hate you, don't leave me.* I also saw fleeting hints of personality disorders in #5, including narcissism, histrionics, borderline as well. Ultimately, he filed divorce papers. I spent five years heartbroken, sometimes to the point of catatonia and suicidal thoughts.

I don't hate men, I really don't. But my reactions to them have certainly led to a lot of depression in my life.

The other day I heard an interview on NPR with Kenny Rogers. It surprised me that he would be on the show. He never seemed that special or interesting to me. I think even the interviewer—Leonard Lopate—sounded disdainful at some of Kenny's answers, as I was.

I learned that Kenny's been married six times. He's now 74 and on wife #6, with whom he has two twin boys age eight.

I don't have any trouble committing, he said during the interview, laughing.

He said, *There is a fine line between being driven to succeed and being selfish. I crossed that line.*

My gut twisted when he added, *I loved every one of my wives.*

This is the stuff I sometimes hate about some men.

Kenny blamed his divorces on the fact that he spent a good part of his life touring the world. What he didn't say, but I suspect, is that his wives stayed home and raised his seven children.

Next week, he said during the interview, *I will go to Singapore to tour.* His current, and I assume much younger, wife will stay home to raise their twin boys.

One more thing about Kenny: He was on the radio plugging his new book. He said his first book had lots of photographs of famous people: Elizabeth Taylor. Michael Jackson. Four Presidents.

Leonard Lopate, noting that Kenny had met presidents of both political parties, asked if it was easy for him to maintain a nonpartisan stance. *Oh yes,* Kenny answered, in a voice meant to be charming, *honestly I didn't even know what party each President belonged to. I'm a guy who likes to get involved with the concept more than the people.* He must have felt that way about marriage, too.

It takes a while but I always get over, at least on some level, the uncomfortable feelings that came with each of my unwanted break-ups. Though I also know they are embedded so deeply they will never disappear completely.

Last Sunday was a case in point. I experienced in one day a speeded-up version of the unhealthy patterns set by my relationships with #1-5.

A year ago, my neighbor's wife died. They had, I believe, a good 30-year marriage. They were, I believe, monogamous.

I live in a very conservative town. The fact that my neighbors were former hippies—who had even lived for a while in Steamboat Springs—made me happy.

After Ellen died, I knew Randy grieved. I answered his emails and phone calls, even asked him if he'd like to go out to dinner a few times. These weren't dates, but he always drove and paid and kissed me on the cheek when he dropped me back home.

Then a friend urged him to go on Match. We compared notes on our dates, laughing. I told him about the guy who told me he liked working on his Jaguar and Porsche and other cars but when I asked if he also liked to drive them said, *Oh no, these are Matchbox cars.*

Good Lord, I thought, *what am I doing out here?*

Randy told me about the woman who said she was 61 but was really 75. I considered Randy a friend, though also a man who would have interested me if I had not known his wife and known that he was a very new widower.

Then last weekend, Randy emailed on a Saturday night asking what I was doing. I said nothing. I'd actually just left the kitchen when my father's favorite show, Lawrence Welk, came on. My parents, who had moved into my house after my divorce, sat at the table holding hands.

I said to Randy, *Do you want to come watch a movie?*

When he came to the house, we went downstairs to use the big TV. I found the right remote and was pushing buttons when he said, *I can think of something better to do than watch TV.*

Our clothes came off quickly. It surprised me how good, even how familiar it felt to be touched, kissed, licked. It surprised me that my body really hadn't abandoned me. And, after about half an hour, it surprised me when Randy said, *I love sex. I want to have sex with everyone I can.*

I don't know what I'd been hoping for. Hope wasn't even in my vocabulary any more. Nor was the word relationship. But right away, as soon as he said that, my stomach dropped. I wanted him to go home, and I wanted to go into my own bedroom to watch TV or not watch TV by myself.

But I faked it.

I brushed my hair back from my eyes and looked at him, stupidly smiling, and said, even with a little laugh, *So this is just a booty call?* I wanted to show that I was cool with anything. I wanted to show that I knew we were getting up there in age, or rather actually already *were* up there in age, and life is short, and seize the day and all that good stuff.

I laughed though I really didn't feel like laughing. The first therapist I ever saw asked me why I was smiling when I was telling him sad things. At that point I would have been telling him about the suicide of #1 and the abortion and the disappearance of #2. But I didn't want to be a downer.

In the same way, I faked it with Randy. We kept kissing and doing other stuff for a few more minutes and finally I said, I'm really tired, and got him to leave. I didn't want to hurt his feelings.

I don't remember exactly what Randy said when I asked if this was a booty call. And at this point I don't think he really qualifies as a #6. What I do know is that although hope proper isn't in my vocabulary anymore, some days, when I see Mom and Dad sitting on the couch together or holding hands, I want to imagine a day when I can stop counting.

ABOUT THE AUTHOR

Donna Baier Stein's writing has appeared in *Virginia Quarterly Review,* *Kansas Quarterly, Prairie Schooner, Washingtonian,* and many other journals and anthologies. She has been a Finalist in the Iowa Fiction Awards, a Johns Hopkins University Writing Seminars Fellowship, Bread Loaf Scholarship, a grant from the New Jersey Council of the Arts, prizes from the Poetry Council of Virginia, two Pushcart nominations, and an Honorable Mention in the 2013 Allen E. Ginsberg Poetry Awards. Her as-yet unpublished novel received the PEN/New England Discovery Award for Fiction. Her poetry chapbook *Sometimes You Sense the Difference* was published in 2012. Donna was a Founding Editor of *Bellevue Literary Review* and founded and currently publishes *TIFERET.* She is also an award-winning direct response copywriter. www.donnabaierstein.com.

ABOUT THE COVER ARTIST

Alexandra Eldridge, born of artist parents, received her BA in Art and Literature at Ohio University. She has continued her education at Cambridge University, England; Santa Reparata Graphic Workshop in Florence, Italy; Penland College, and most recently The Photographers Formulary in Montana. Alexandra co-founded an establishment for the arts, Golgonooza, based on the philosophies of Wm. Blake.

She has had over 40 solo shows and has participated in many group shows throughout the U.S. and abroad: Paris, London, Belgrade, New York, California, Santa Fe.

Alexandra has been commissioned to paint murals in the Place des Vosges, Paris, and her work has been used on the cover of eight books of poetry. Traveling, as an important part of her inspiration, has taken her to Artists Residencies on the Island of Elba, Italy and the Valparaiso Foundation in Almeria, Spain.

Art News, *Art on Paper*, *New American Painting*, and *One Hundred Painters of the Southwest* are just a few of the publications Alexandra has been featured in.

Alexandra Eldridge is collected by the likes of William Hurt, Steve Buscemi and Edie Falco besides many other prestigious collections.

ABOUT THE COVER DESIGNER

Allen Mohr is a graphic designer who loves reading books as much as designing them. He lives in New York, where he has made a long career of putting intriguing images with captivating words in a broad range of media.

Proof